"Would you come here?" Shane asked in a soft tone.

A wave of longing washed through her. Darci recognized the danger, but she was so tempted.

His voice was deep, persuasive. "Nobody takes off their clothes, and no hands below the waist."

"Can you stick to those rules?"

"I can if you can."

"I can." She had no choice.

He smiled. Heart thudding, she took the three steps that brought her in front of him. He reached for her hand and drew her into his arms.

She knew she shouldn't relax. Still, she couldn't help herself. Just for a few minutes, she promised. Darci felt the strength and the intimacy of his body pressed to hers. It was taut and sexy, and absolutely forbidden.

* * *

Sex, Lies and the CEO is part of the Chicago Sons series: Men who work hard, love harder and live with their fathers' legacies...

Dear Reader,

Writing the Chicago Sons series is an opportunity to explore the idea of family secrets. I think almost everyone has one, or two, or three. When they are revealed, it can be a cause for consternation or celebration. Hopefully, most are a cause for celebration.

In book one, *Sex, Lies and the CEO*, aerospace billionaire CEO Shane Colborn is battling scandals in the public eye, trying to save the reputation of his company. Little does he know that Darci Rivers has learned the secret that can bring down his empire. Darci is determined to reveal the dark truth behind Colborn Aerospace, and she's willing to go to any lengths to get it—spying, lying, even dating the disreputable Shane Colborn. But up close, Shane's not what she'd expected. She's falling for him, even as her deception unravels around her.

I hope you enjoy Shane and Darci's clash of wills.

Happy reading!

Barbara Dunlop

SEX, LIES AND THE CEO

BARBARA DUNLOP

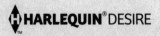

Recycling programs
for this product may
not exist in your area.

ISBN-13: 978-0-373-73389-7

Sex, Lies and the CEO

Copyright © 2015 by Barbara Dunlop

Printed in U.S.A.

Barbara Dunlop writes romantic stories while curled up in a log cabin in Canada's far north, where bears outnumber people and it snows six months of the year. Fortunately she has a brawny husband and two teenage children to haul firewood and clear the driveway while she sips cocoa and muses about her upcoming chapters. Barbara loves to hear from readers. You can contact her through her website, barbaradunlop.com.

Books by Barbara Dunlop

HARLEQUIN DESIRE

An After-Hours Affair
A Golden Betrayal
A Conflict of Interest
The Missing Heir

Colorado Cattle Barons

A Cowboy Comes Home
A Cowboy in Manhattan
An Intimate Bargain
Millionaire in a Stetson
A Cowboy's Temptation
The Last Cowboy Standing

Chicago Sons

Sex, Lies and the CEO

Visit the Author Profile page at Harlequin.com
or barbaradunlop.com for more titles!

For my son

One

"Don't answer that," Darci Rivers called out, rushing across the hardwood floor of the cluttered loft apartment.

"It's not going to be him," said Jennifer Shelton as she dug into her purse.

Darci slid on sock feet around a pile of packing boxes while the phone jangled again. "It's him."

"It's not—" Jennifer glanced at the display on her phone. Then she looked up at Darci. "It's him."

Darci deftly scooped the phone from her roommate's hand. "You *will not* give in."

"I won't give in." Even as she spoke, Jennifer cast a longing glance at the phone.

"He's dead to you," said Darci, waving the phone for emphasis as she backed a safe distance away.

"Maybe he's—"

"He's not."

"You don't know what I was about to say."

Darci hit the end button to cancel the call and tucked the phone into the front pocket of her jeans. "You were going to say 'maybe he's sorry.'"

Jennifer pursed her lips together. "Maybe he is."

Darci angled for the kitchen area of the open-concept space. A sloped wall of glass stretched up beside her, overlooking the distant Chicago skyline. Skylights decorated the high ceiling, while two lofts bracketed either end of the spacious, rectangular room.

The phone rang again, vibrating inside her pocket.

"Give it back," said Jennifer, following behind.

Darci rounded the end of the island counter. "What was it you said to me last night?"

"It could be a client."

"*What* was it you said to me?"

"*Darci.*"

"If it's a client, they'll leave a message."

It was nearly seven o'clock on a Tuesday night. Though Darci and Jennifer prided themselves on being easily available to clients of their web-design business, it wouldn't kill them to miss one call.

"What kind of customer service is that?"

Darci pulled the phone out of her pocket to check the display. "It's him." She declined the call and tucked the phone away.

"Something could be wrong," said Jennifer, taking another step.

Darci couldn't help but smile at that. "Of course something's wrong. He only just realized you were serious."

On the counter, she located a packing box labeled "wine rack" and peeled it open. She'd wisely packed the corkscrew with the wine bottles for easy access after the move. Now, if she could only remember which carton held the glasses.

She pointed at another box on the island. "Check the white one."

"You can't hold my phone hostage."

"Sure I can. You made me swear I would."

"I've changed my mind."

"No backsies."

"That's ridiculous."

"You said, and I quote, *don't ever let me talk to that son-of-a-bitch again.* I think the wineglasses are in the white box."

Jennifer clamped her jaw.

Giving up, Darci reached out and pulled the carton closer to her, stripping off the wide packing tape. "He cheated on you, Jen."

"He was drunk."

"He's going to get drunk again, and he's going to cheat on you again. You don't even know if that was the first time."

"I'm pretty sure—"

"Pretty sure? Listen to yourself. You need to be 100 percent positive he never has and never will, or else you have to walk."

"You are so idealistic."

"Aha." Darci had located the wineglasses. She extracted a pair of them and turned to the sink to give them a rinse.

"Nobody can ever know for sure," said Jennifer.

"Are you listening to yourself?"

There was a long silence before Jennifer spoke. "I'm trying hard not to."

Darci grinned as she shook water droplets from the wet glasses. "There you go. Welcome back, girl."

She turned back to the breakfast bar, and Jennifer slid up onto one of the counter stools. "He's just so…"

"Self-centered?"

"I was thinking *hot*." Jennifer absently bent back the flaps of the cardboard box closest to her.

"There has to be more to a man than buff pecs and a tight butt."

Jennifer gave a shrug as she peered into the depths of the box.

"Tell me I'm right," said Darci.

"You're right."

"Say it like you mean it."

Jennifer drew a heavy sigh and extracted a stack of old photo albums, setting them on the countertop. "I mean it. Can I have my phone back?"

"No. But you can have a big glass of this ten-dollar merlot."

The two women had consumed plenty of cheap wine together. They'd been best friends since high school and had both won scholarships to Columbia, in graphic design. They'd roomed together for four years, sharing opinions, jokes and secrets.

Darci would trust Jennifer with her life, but not with Ashton Watson.

Her best friend had a weak spot when it came to the smooth-talking charmer. She'd dumped him three times in the past four months, but each time he'd waxed eloquent, swearing he'd be more thoughtful, less self-centered. And each time, she'd taken him back.

Darci wasn't about to let it happen again. The man had no clue how to be in a couple.

Jennifer extracted three thick manila envelopes from a box in front of her and set them beside the photo albums. "I'm not thirsty."

"Yes, you are." Darci pushed one of the glasses across the wide counter.

Jennifer dug down and removed a worn leather wallet from the box, then turned the case over in her hands. "This is your dad's stuff?"

"It's from his top dresser drawer." Darci gazed at the small collection of her father's things. "I packed it away when I cleared out his apartment. I was too emotional to look through it that day."

Jennifer looked worried. "You want me to leave it alone?"

Darci knew there was no point in procrastinating any longer. She perched on the other stool and took a bracing sip of the wine. "I'm ready. It's been three months."

Jennifer reached back into the carton and came up with an old wooden box.

"Cigars?" she asked.

"I only ever saw him smoke cigarettes."

"It looks pretty old." Jennifer sniffed at the wood. "Cedar."

The lid was secured with a small brass clasp, and she slipped it free.

Darci felt more curious than distressed. She still missed her father every day, but he'd been sick and in pain for many months before his death. And though she didn't know all the details, she knew he'd been in emotional pain for years, likely since her mother had taken off when Darci was a baby. She was beginning to accept that he was finally at peace.

Jennifer raised the lid.

Darci leaned in to look.

"Money," said Jennifer.

The revelation confused Darci.

"Coins." Jennifer lifted a row of plastic sleeves containing gold-and-silver coins. "It looks like a collection."

"I sure hope they're not valuable."

"Why would you hope that?"

"He struggled for years to make ends meet. I'd hate to think he deprived himself and saved these for me."

"He was still buying single malt," said Jennifer.

Darci couldn't help but smile at the memory. Born and raised in Aberdeen, Ian Rivers swore by a strong, peaty Scotch.

"What's this?" Jennifer pulled a folded envelope from beneath the coins. A photograph was tucked in the fold, and she drew it out.

Darci checked the picture. "That's definitely my dad."

Ian was standing in a small, sparse office, his hand braced on a wooden desk. She flipped the photo, but nothing was written on the back.

Jennifer opened the unsealed envelope.

"A coin appraisal?" Darci guessed, taking a sip of her wine.

"A letter."

"To my dad?"

It must have had significant sentimental value. Darci couldn't help but wonder if it was a love letter. She even dared to hope it was from her mother, Alison. Though Alison Rivers had never contacted them, it would be nice to think she might have thought about them once in a while.

"It's *from* your dad. To someone named Dalton Colborn."

Darci's stomach did a flip. She hadn't heard the name in years.

Jennifer glanced up at the silence. "You know him?"

"I never met him. He owned Colborn Aerospace. And he was once my Dad's business partner."

"Your dad was involved in *Colborn Aerospace*?"

"It was a different company they had together, D&I Holdings. I don't know much about it, and it all ended when I was just a baby." Darci gazed at the picture. "Dalton and my dad were both engineers. They opened a company together, but it all fell apart, apparently quite badly. For as long as I can remember, Dad would fly into a rage whenever he saw the Colborn name."

"There's a thirty-two-cent stamp on it," said Jennifer. "Never mind old, that's ancient. It was never mailed."

The flap on the envelope gaped open.

"Read it," said Darci.

"You sure?"

Darci slugged back a swallow of wine. "I'm sure."

Shane Colborn sent the fuchsia hardcover skittering across his wide cherrywood desk. Justin Massey, head of the legal department at Colborn Aerospace, trapped it before it could drop to the floor.

"Well, that's a new low," said Shane.

He hated reading about himself. Business articles were bad enough. The tabloids were worse, but they were mercifully short. This mess was appalling.

"There's no way to stop it from being released," said Justin. "We were lucky to get our hands on this copy." He paused. "So, how much of it is true?"

Shane struggled to clear the anger from his brain. "I don't know. Are you looking for a number?"

"Sure. Give me a number."

"Twenty, maybe thirty percent. The dates and places and events are all accurate. But I sure don't talk like an eighteenth-century poet in bed."

Justin's face broke into a grin.

"Shut up," Shane ordered.

"I never said a word."

Shane pushed back his leather desk chair and stood, his anger level rising instead of falling. "I didn't flirt with other women when she was in the room. And cheap? *Cheap?* I don't think the woman glanced at a price tag the entire time we were dating. Limos, restaurants, clothes, parties. I bought her a blue-diamond bracelet for her birthday last March."

It was a purchase he now regretted. He didn't mind the cost, but there was something intimate about diamonds, particularly those in a custom setting. But Bianca had pouted and whined prettily until he'd given in. He had to admit, no matter how ugly this breakup became, he was relieved to be out from under her complaining.

"I'm most worried about chapter six," said Justin.

"Where she accuses me of collusion and corporate espionage?"

"Clients really don't care what you're like in bed. But they do care if you're price-fixing or stealing their intellectual property."

"I'm not."

"I know you're not."

It was reassuring for Shane to hear that his lawyer trusted him. "It sounded like you wanted me to answer that."

"I'm not the one you have to convince."

Shane nodded at the book with the crass cover. "Is there a way for me to rebut?"

"Not unless you want a he-said-she-said battle in the media. You know Bianca will do all the local talk shows. Any move you make prolongs the story."

"So I stay silent."

"Yes."

"And let them think I'm a pansy in the sack?"

"I'll be advising our clients that the espionage and collusion accusations are ridiculous. I could mention your sex life, if you'd like."

"You're a real comedian."

"I try. Have you heard anything from Gobrecht this week?"

Shane shook his head.

Gobrecht Airlines was headquartered in Berlin, and they were in the final stages of awarding a contract for twenty new commuter jets. The Colborn Aware 200 was the front runner. If Gobrecht made a commitment to buy, Beaumont Air in Paris was likely to follow suit with an even larger contract.

Justin backed toward the office door. "I know your public profile has always been good for business. But can you please try to stay out of the headlines for a while?"

"I've never tried to get into them. I thought Bianca knew the score."

Bianca had been introduced to Shane by the Millers. She was the daughter of their good friend, so Shane had assumed she'd grown up around wealthy, high-profile people. It never occurred to him that she'd gossip in public. And it sure never occurred to him that she'd write a supposed tell-all book for money.

"It's impossible to know who to trust," said Justin.

"I trust you."

"I'm contractually obligated to be trustworthy."

"Maybe that's what I should do next time." Shane was only half joking. "Have my dates sign a nondisclosure agreement before the appetizers."

"It might be better if you don't date for a while."

"That doesn't sound like much fun."

"Read a book. Take up a hobby."

"Like golf or fishing?"

"Not a lot of fishing in the greater Chicago area. But you could golf."

"Tried it once. I'd have to hang myself." Shane shuddered at the memory.

"You do know it's not about the ball. It's about the conversation."

"Boring people play golf."

Justin paused beside the closed door. "Powerful people play golf."

"I'd rather scuba dive or target shoot."

"Go for it."

Shane had considered both of those things, dreaming of a long weekend in the Keys or a rustic lodge in Montana. "It's a little hard to find the time."

"Now that you've given up dating, you'll have nothing but time on your hands."

"There's a board meeting on Friday. We break ground on the new wing of the R & D facility Wednesday morning. Then I'm hosting the search-and-rescue fundraiser at the mansion next Saturday night." Shane paused. "And I'm not going stag to that."

"Sure you are."

"Uh, no, I'm not."

"Then find a nice, safe date," said Justin. "Take your cousin."

"Madeline is *not* going to be my date to the fundraiser."

"Why not? She could be your hostess. It's not the same as a date."

"That's pathetic. I'm not going to look pathetic at my own party."

"You won't look pathetic. You'll look shrewd. The trick here is to give the media *absolutely nothing* to report."

"You don't think they'll report that I'm dating my cousin?"

"They'll report that you and Madeline were impeccable hosts and that Colborn raised hundreds of thousands for the search-and-rescue service."

Shane's instinct was to argue. But he forced himself to think it through. Was cohosting with Madeline really the safe route?

He knew she'd do it for him. She was a sweetheart. Would it deflect public criticism? More importantly, would it protect his privacy?

Justin spoke up again. "There's a fine line between keeping your company in the public eye and becoming a social-media spectacle."

"I've crossed it, haven't I?"

"Bianca crossed it for you."

Shane capitulated. "Fine. I'll call Maddie."

"Good decision."

"You do know I have a 100 percent success rate, getting lucky after that particular party."

"You do know those women are sleeping with the billionaire persona and not the man, right?"

"The family mansion has to be good for something."

The Barrington Hills house had been in his family for decades. But it was an hour commute to downtown. And what single man needed fourteen acres and seven bedrooms?

Shane mostly lived at his Lake Shore Drive penthouse—

three bedrooms, a fantastic view and close to any number of fine restaurants.

"I'm sure your father would be proud of how you're using the family assets," Justin drawled.

Shane couldn't help but smile at the memory. His dad had been gone for six years now, tragically killed along with Shane's mother in a boating accident when Shane was twenty-four. He missed them both. And although Justin was being sarcastic, Dalton wouldn't have had the slightest problem with Shane's love life.

Shane heard his assistant, Ginger, over the intercom. "Mr. Colburn? A Hans Strutz is on the phone from Gobrecht Airlines."

He and Justin exchanged a worried look.

Shane reached out to press the intercom button on his desk phone. "I'll pick it up."

"Thank you, sir. Line one."

"Thanks, Ginger." He took a bracing breath. "Well, this could be really good or really bad."

Justin reached for the door handle. "Call me when you're done."

"I will." Shane punched line one.

Darci sat perched on a bus-stop bench across the busy street from the Colborn Aerospace headquarters. The June sunshine glinted on the giant royal blue sign, which stretched across the front of the building. The twenty-one story structure was two blocks from the river, overlooking a small park.

Her father's unmailed letter had been a revelation. It explained Ian's bitterness, his rages at Dalton Colborn and likely his fondness for Scotch, which had increased as the years went by. The letter accused Dalton of betraying Ian, of stealing and patenting her father's next-generation turbine design.

It seemed Ian and Dalton had been best friends for years, until Dalton got greedy and stole everything for himself. Ian's letter had threatened a lawsuit. He wanted money, sure. But he also wanted professional recognition for his invention. Dal-

ton had won a prestigious award for the turbine, gaining fame
that had translated into wealth and skyrocketing growth for
Colborn Aerospace, while Ian's marriage had broken up and
he had spiraled into depression and obscurity.

The letter stated that there was irrefutable proof of Ian's
claim in the company's records. He said his original, signed
schematic drawings were hidden away in a place where only
he could find them. He'd wanted a court order to retrieve the
designs and force Dalton to come clean.

But the letter was never mailed. And Darci could only guess
at the reasons her father might have changed his mind. Maybe
he hadn't wanted to tip Dalton off, to risk Dalton finding the
drawings and destroying them. If so, why hadn't he called a
lawyer? Or maybe he had.

She realized she'd probably never know.

Now she sat staring at the Colborn Aerospace building and
wondered if the proof could possibly be inside. Were there papers moldering in a basement filing cabinet that showed her
father was a brilliant engineer? If there were, how could she
get her hands on them?

She watched people walk in and out of the building, alone,
in pairs, in groups. Some were obviously executives and office staff. Some were maintenance workers. Some were likely
clients and customers.

She could walk into the lobby right now, and nobody would
stop her. Though there was probably security to keep her from
getting much farther than that. Maybe she'd ask to see Shane
Colborn. Maybe she'd march right up to him and demand to
see the historical files.

Then again, maybe that would be stupid. Shane was likely
as selfish and greedy as his father. If he learned there was
proof of his family's dishonesty, there was no way he'd let her
hunt for it. Instead, he'd be the one to find it and destroy it.

A bus rolled along the curb. Its air brakes groaned as it
came to a stop and blocked her view. A few people stepped off
while others boarded, then it pulled away, diesel engine grind-
ing loudly before the sounds mingled with the other traffic.

Children squealed in the park beside her. Birds swooped from aspens to maple trees. The wind freshened the air, blowing away the exhaust from the four-lane thoroughfare.

It was lunchtime, and hundreds of people moved through the park and along the sidewalks. More entered the Colborn building. More came out.

Staring at the imposing stone structure, Darci knew the smart thing to do was walk away. She should forget the letter existed and carry on with her regular life. She could head back to her car, return to the loft and finish unpacking her belongings.

It was Friday. She and Jennifer were going to the Woodrow Club tonight. They'd meet up with some friends from Columbia, have a few drinks, maybe run into some nice guys. Who knew? This could be the night she met her soul mate.

Not that she was necessarily fixating on meeting Mr. Right. She'd like to get married someday, settle down, have kids. Who wouldn't? But she was in no hurry.

Her and Jennifer's web-design business was growing at a very satisfying pace. They'd planned a vacation in New York City for July. They had reservations at a hotel on Times Square and tickets to three shows. It was going to be fantastic.

Another bus passed, but it didn't stop.

She gazed over the tops of the cars and taxis, staring at the glass doors that led to the Colborn Aerospace lobby, while speculating on what kind of a person could get access to the basement. A repairman, perhaps. She could rent a uniform, buy a toolbox and pretend she was from the telephone or the electric company.

Too bad she didn't know a fuse from a resistor.

Maybe she could deliver a pizza.

A woman headed up the stairs to the front doors, then paused to smooth her skirt, seeming to brace herself before reaching for the door handle. She looked young, nervous and self-conscious.

Job interview, Darci concluded.

Then she sat up straight, a lightning bolt flashing in her brain.

Job interview.

Employees of Colborn Aerospace could wander all over the building. They would have security access, possibly even door keys. Nobody would question their right to be there. And they could chat up the other employees, find out where company records were kept, browse through them under one pretext or another, probably find anything they wanted about the company's history.

That was the answer. She'd apply for a job, go to work for Colborn. It was a brilliant plan.

Two

Under normal circumstances, Darci's guilt alone would have stopped her from crashing any party anywhere, never mind one that hosted the who's who of Chicago. But a week into her new job at Colborn Aerospace, she'd learned the oldest records were kept at the Colborn mansion. Tonight was her best chance to look around inside.

She'd rented a four-thousand-dollar, beaded, gold silk evening gown, splurged on a pair of sparkling heels and shelled out a fortune for hair and makeup at the swankiest salon in her neighborhood. If she did say so herself, she looked fabulous. At a passing glance, nobody would guess that she didn't belong among the rich and influential.

Now she just needed to get through the front door.

At the top of the semicircular staircase, a butler was discreetly checking invitations. Darci hovered at the edge of the driveway, wondering how best to approach him, but she didn't dare stand still too long or she'd call attention to herself.

A gray-haired couple brushed past her. The woman was dressed in a dramatic peacock-blue gown with a diamond brooch at the shoulder. Making a split-second decision, Darci fell into step beside the woman.

"That's a lovely brooch," she said to her as they walked.

Luckily, the woman turned and gave her a friendly smile. "Thank you. It's Cartier."

Darci frowned. "Oh dear. You have a little crease." She boldly reached to the fabric above the brooch, pretending to smooth it out.

"May I confirm your invitation, sir," the butler said to the older man.

Darci's heart thudded as the man handed him a card.

"Nice of you to join us, Mr. Saunders," said the butler.

"There we go," Darci said to the woman, keeping her gaze

studiously fixed on the dress, pretending she was part of the Saunders party. "That looks much better."

"Thank you." The woman, obviously Mrs. Saunders, nodded her appreciation.

Another couple stepped up behind them, drawing the butler's attention, and Darci quickly moved forward.

Her heart was still thudding wildly as they went through the stately front doors and into the huge foyer.

"Enjoy your evening," she managed to say to Mrs. Saunders.

"Enjoy yours," Mrs. Saunders replied.

Darci peeled off to the right, anxious to mix in with the nearest crowd.

"Champagne, ma'am?" asked a neatly uniformed waiter.

"Thank you." Darci helped herself to a crystal flute from his tray.

She had no intention of consuming any alcohol, but holding the glass would make her look more like a genuine guest.

Earlier in the week, she'd started a job in the records department of Colborn Aerospace. It was an entry-level position, requiring little in the way of experience, with a very low pay rate.

But for her, it was perfect, because it gave her access to the basement of the building. She and Jennifer had then poured over her father's few belongings, hoping for a clue to the location of the original turbine-design drawings. Unfortunately, they hadn't found anything else that seemed to help.

But during her company orientation, Darci learned that some of the historical records were stored in the basement of the mansion. So when she read about the search-and-rescue fundraiser, she threw together this plan.

As the guests milled around her in the main reception room, she took an absentminded sip of the champagne. So far, so good.

"Good evening." A thirty-something man in a business suit approached her.

"Good evening," Darci returned, mustering a friendly smile.

He offered his hand. "I'm Lawrence Tucker, Tucker Transportation."

"Darci." She hesitated for a split second, realizing she shouldn't use her real name. "Lake."

"Nice to meet you Darci Lake. You're a supporter of the search-and-rescue program?"

"Very much so. And you?"

His handshake was firm, his attitude forthright. He was a fairly attractive man, tall, with broad shoulders that gave him a powerful stance.

"Tucker Transportation donated twenty containers of freight shipping to anywhere in Europe." He indicated a long row of tables with silent-auction signage above them.

"You ship to Europe?" She wanted to keep the conversation focused on him and away from her.

"We ship worldwide. Europe, Africa, Asia, Pacific."

"You're a large company?"

"You've never heard of Tucker Transportation?"

"I've definitely heard of you," she quickly lied. "But I'm afraid I don't know many details."

"We're the third-largest shipping company in the nation."

"Impressive." She took another sip of her champagne.

"There you are, Tuck." A tall, gorgeous blonde woman twined her arm possessively around Lawrence Tucker's.

"Hello, Petra." He greeted her with a quick peck on the cheek.

She pouted her deep red lips. "Don't forget, you promised to come with me on a wine-cellar tour."

"I haven't forgotten."

The woman's gaze moved to Darci, where it paused, becoming speculative.

"This is Darci Lake," said Tuck.

"Nice to meet you," said Petra. She didn't let go of Tuck. If anything, she pressed closer.

She was several inches taller than Darci and wearing four-inch heels. Darci guessed she was in her late twenties. Her manicure was perfect, as was her hair. And her gown likely cost more than Darci's. Plus, she probably owned it.

"It was nice to meet you," Darci said to Tuck, not having the slightest desire to get between Petra and her designs on the man. "Perhaps I'll see you again later on."

As she moved toward the back of the house, Darci left the great room behind and found herself in a wide open hall. It had twenty-foot ceilings, marble pillars and gleaming white archways. Antique-style lampposts dotted the perimeter, while an imposing wrought-iron chandelier hung in the center of the room. The decor focused on an equestrian theme, with a big bronze statue of a stallion on a large rough-hewn wood table. Rich oil paintings of rural stables and the countryside hung on the walls, and several red velvet-and-walnut armchairs bordered the room.

After an initial scan of the area, Darci found her attention drawn to a small open doorway. It led to a staircase, tucked in a corner behind a pillar and partially screened by one of the lampposts.

She wandered toward it, pretending to be fascinated by a grandfather clock against the wall. Feeling like a spy, she glanced around to see if anyone was paying attention to her movements.

The crowds were sparser here than out front in the great room. But there were enough people that she blended.

She eased her way behind the lamp.

Then she moved to the pillar.

With another quick check to make sure no one was watching, she scooted to the shadowed staircase and started down.

The stairwell was dim, and she gripped the rail. After what seemed like a long distance, she came out at a narrow white-walled hallway with a blue-and-silver-tiled floor and fluorescent lights along the ceiling.

Her heart began pounding harder as she chose between left and right. Right would take her to the back of the house while left would take her toward the front. It was a toss-up, but it seemed to her that decades-old business records would more likely be at the rear of the house.

She turned right and started along the hall.

She came to a closed door and tried the knob. It was locked. She jiggled it, thinking it was old and it might give way.

"Can I help you with something?" came a deep, accusatory voice.

She quickly twisted around, and her heart sank with a thud. His face was shadowed, but she instantly recognized him.

She swallowed. "Mr. Colborn."

He took a step forward, his piercing blue eyes pinning her in place. "Did you take a wrong turn?"

Her mind scrambled for a plausible explanation. "I, uh...I heard you were giving a wine-cellar tour."

His eyes narrowed. "You did, did you?"

"Petra mentioned it. Petra and Tuck. I was talking to them earlier, and—"

"You know Tuck?"

Darci nodded. She'd known Tuck for all of five minutes. But she wasn't about to get stuck on that detail.

Shane Colborn seemed to relax a bit. "I haven't seen him yet tonight."

"Petra found him. And, well, she didn't seem to want to share."

Shane cracked a smile. "She doesn't. She's had her sights set on him since we were teenagers."

He moved closer still, offering his hand. "I'm Shane Colborn, the host of the party. Well, me and my cousin Madeline are the hosts."

Darci immediately accepted the handshake. "I know who you are. I'm Darci Lake. You have a remarkable home."

"Remarkable *appealing*, or remarkable *ostentatious*?"

"A little of both," she answered before she thought it through. She realized her words had sounded like a criticism. "I mean, it's wonderful, of course. It's just that I can't imagine—"

"Living here?"

"It is intimidating," she answered honestly.

His furrowed brow told her she was blowing the entire conversation.

Insulting his home was the last thing she wanted to do. "I didn't mean it the way it came out." She gave her head a brief shake. "Can I please start over?"

"Go for it."

She braced herself. "It's a phenomenal home. And I'm sure you love it here. But it's more opulent than I'm used to, so it's hard to imagine living in it."

"That wasn't a bad recovery."

"Thank you."

"Personally, I also find it intimidating. And I grew up here."

"So, you were just messing with me?"

"I was," he said.

"That wasn't a very nice thing to do."

"I found you skulking around my basement, trying to break into a locked room. I don't think it's my behavior that deserves criticism."

She could have kicked herself for bringing the conversation back to what she was doing down here. But to her surprise, he offered his arm.

"Would you still like to see the wine cellar?"

"I would," she quickly answered.

"The official tour is scheduled for later on, and I have some terrific wines lined up. But we can get a head start."

She slipped her hand into the crook of his elbow. He was steady and sure. Her thumb brushed his biceps and found it defined and hard as iron.

"Do you prefer Old World wines or New World wines?" he asked as they came toward the front of the mansion.

"New World," she answered, though it was just a stab in the dark. She knew nothing about wines but the color and the price.

"So, not a snob?"

"Not a snob," she agreed easily.

"People seem all excited about malbecs. But give me a solid

cabernet sauvignon any day of the week. What about you? Cab sauv? Or maybe pinot noir?

"Cabernet sauvignon," she told him, to be agreeable.

"You're lying."

How could he tell? "I'm not."

"Then you're being polite."

"That would be a change of pace."

He gave a low chuckle. It was a very appealing sound.

She caught herself glancing at his profile.

He was an astonishingly handsome man. She'd already known that from his many pictures in the media. But the pictures hadn't done him justice. Some tabloids called him Chicago's most eligible bachelor, and she wasn't about to argue the point.

What woman wouldn't fantasize about being held in his strong arms and kissing those full lips? Add to that his wealth and his standing in the business community, and she could understand why the elite ladies of Chicago were taking turns as his date.

They passed another closed door, and she remembered why she was here. She needed to stay focused.

"What's in there?" she asked of the closed door.

He gave her a puzzled look. "In where?"

She backed off, realizing she could easily arouse his suspicions again. "Besides the wine cellar, what do people keep in a great big basement like this?"

He gave a glance around the hallway. "Good question. The only place I ever go is the wine cellar, being a playboy bachelor."

"Now who's lying?"

His father might have been dishonorable, but a man didn't run a billion-dollar company by being nothing but a playboy. She didn't buy for a minute that he'd never looked through his own basement.

"Some antique furniture," he said. "Boxes of things from my parents, probably some art and some silverware. There are no bodies, if that's what you're asking."

"It wasn't. But now that you mention it…" She made a show of gazing worriedly over her shoulder.

"We are all alone down here." He finished her thought in a theatrical voice.

"Are you trustworthy, Mr. Colborn?"

"Not even a little bit. Here we are."

He stopped in front of a wide oak door with a thick, twisted wrought-iron handle and long black hinges, strapping the aged planks together. Stonework bracketed the door on both sides, giving the entry an unfortunate dungeon look.

He extracted a long key and inserted it into a deadbolt lock.

For a horrible second, she wondered if he somehow knew who she was and if she ought to be afraid of him.

"An estate this size has a lot of staff," he said as he turned the key. "Some of them are transient. And my father collected some ridiculously valuable wines."

The door swung open with a groan.

Darci peered inside the dark room. "So, this isn't the place where you lock up the innocent young women caught trespassing."

Shane pointed with his thumb. "That room is farther down the hall."

"Good to know."

He flicked a light switch, and a massive room came into view. Stone walls stretched back farther than she could see. A huge rectangular wooden table sat in the center of the room, with at least twenty chairs surrounding it. The ceiling was beamed with heavy timbers, supported by thick pillars. Gleaming cedar racks and shelves stretched along each wall, with more rows protruding behind the table.

The room was cold, the scent of cedar hanging in the still air. Most bottles were on their sides in the racks. But some were out on display, while numerous stemmed glasses of varying shapes and sizes hung inverted above the table.

"This is incredible," she whispered, taking a step into the room and turning around to take it all in.

"Incredible *charming* or incredible *intimidating*?" he asked.

"Awe inspiring."

Everyone who visited the cellar must have the same reaction.

She moved inside, gazing in amazement. "It makes me want to learn more about wine."

"What would you like to learn?"

She turned to face him. "What's good?"

He drew back in obvious surprise. "Seriously?"

"For starters."

"I was expecting a much more specific question."

"Okay. What *tastes* good?"

"In a New World cabernet sauvignon?"

"You were right," she said. "I was playing along back there. I don't know anything about wine."

She realized she'd have to continue sleuthing as soon as possible. But, for now, it seemed best to see this particular charade through to the end.

There was a twinkle in his blue eyes. "Okay." He pulled out one of the chairs. "Then have a seat."

She did as he asked, and he leaned down as he pushed in the chair.

"We'll stick with New World," he said, his voice close to her ear.

She found herself inhaling his fresh scent.

"No point in making you a snob if you're not one already. Pinot noir to start. Then a merlot, cabernet sauvignon and shiraz."

"Four bottles of wine?" Was he joking? "I'll get blasted."

He rose. "We're not going to polish off the bottles."

Of course they weren't. She'd sounded ridiculously unsophisticated. She tried to backtrack. "I only meant tastings usually work better with more people."

"They do," he said. "Want me to go find some?"

She didn't. And that was worrisome. She shouldn't want to stay here alone with Shane. But she did.

His hand gently brushed her shoulder, and the tone of his voice turned intimate. "Me, neither."

Uh-oh.

Before she could formulate a reply, he was gone, moving along the wine racks, perusing the bottles.

She angled her body and watched him from the chair, noting his concentration and the intelligence in his expression as he scrutinized the labels. She'd read he was six feet two. He was obviously in excellent shape. He carried the designer suit with ease across his square shoulders. She could imagine his stomach was washboard hard. She'd already had a chance to feel his biceps.

She knew she couldn't afford to notice, because she couldn't afford any kind of a distraction. But there was no getting around it, Shane Colborn was one sexy package of a man. And it seemed she was as susceptible as the next Chicago woman to his looks and his charm.

Shane realized he was shamefully neglecting his other guests. It was coming up on ten o'clock, and the silent auction was about to close. He knew he should go upstairs and help his cousin Maddie announce the winners, but he wanted to see how Darci felt about the shiraz, the last of their four tastings.

Every time he hosted this fundraiser, he met new people. But few of them fascinated him the way Darci Lake did. She was down-to-earth, unaffected, and he liked her ability to laugh at herself.

She swirled the wine in her oversize glass, checking the color and viscosity as he'd told her. Then she leaned down and inhaled.

"Sharper," she said with a wrinkle of her pert nose.

She was distractingly beautiful, with thick, shoulder-length auburn hair. He guessed she was about five feet six. She was slender, with wonderfully rounded breasts, long legs and delicate hands. Her lips were full, her lashes long and her wide eyes were a startling shade of crystalline green. He could barely keep himself from staring at them.

She took a sip.

Then she nodded decisively. "Sharper. I prefer the cab sauv. Definitely."

"Welcome to the dark side."

Worry flashed through her expression. "Is there something wrong with liking cabernet sauvignon? Am I a bohemian?"

"You have excellent taste in wine."

"Are you just saying that?"

"You like what I like." He replaced her shiraz with a fresh glass of the cab sauv.

She glanced around the tabletop. "We've made a mess."

"It's not so bad."

"You were going to bring people down here for the tasting."

"The staff will clear things up in time."

He checked his watch, knowing he was cutting it pretty tight. For a moment, he considered canceling the tasting, coming up with an excuse to keep everyone else upstairs while he stayed here with Darci.

He gave a silent thank-you to Justin for talking him out of bringing a date tonight. If he played his cards right, perhaps his perfect streak of getting lucky at the search-and-rescue fundraiser would continue. There were hours to go before it ended, and the DJ was about to get things rolling on the dance floor.

Making the decision, he lifted his own wineglass and rose to his feet. "Let's take this with us."

"Sure." She followed his lead. "Where are we going?"

"The dancing's about to start. You want to dance?"

The question seemed to throw her. "With you?"

"Sure, with me. Why not?"

She seemed to scramble. "Uh, you have so many other guests. And you haven't hosted the real wine tasting yet."

He leaned across the table to take her hand. "My cousin Maddie will do the other wine tasting. I've had enough for now."

He kept hold of her hand as they cleared the table and moved through the wine cellar, to the door and out into the hallway.

"Are you going to lock it?" she asked.

"No need. The sommelier will be down in a few minutes."

"You have a sommelier?"

"Doesn't everyone?"

Her steps faltered, and he realized the joke made him sound like a pretentious jerk.

"I'm sorry," he said, stopping them both.

She tipped up her chin to look at him. "Nothing to be sorry about."

"I'm not a spoiled brat. The mansion is purposely equipped for this kind of entertaining. But it's not my regular life."

But a remoteness had entered her eyes. "Your family has a lot of money. That's just the way it is."

"I don't lord it over people, Darci."

"You don't owe me an explanation."

"You're angry."

She looked away. "I'm really not."

But something had changed. He could tell.

"Will you dance with me?" he asked.

She compressed her lips.

"Please dance with me."

Voices traveled down the hall. Shane recognized the accent. The sommelier and his staff were on their way.

She blinked, and whatever had altered her expression was gone. "Okay," she said. "One dance."

He impulsively put an arm around her, his fingertips brushing her shoulder as they resumed walking.

The sommelier, Julien Duval, appeared in the hallway. "Mr. Colborn, sir."

"There's some cleanup needed in the cellar," he told Julien.

"Right away, sir. You'll be joining us?"

"Not this time. Can you find Madeline and ask her to stand in?"

"Of course."

"Thank you, Julien."

Shane followed Darci up the staircase. Her sparkling gold silk dress dipped to a low vee at the back, giving him a marvelous view. It outlined her trim figure and clung enticingly to her backside. He was sorry when they got to the top of the stairs.

He touched his hand to the small of her back, guiding her through the hall to the great room, where the music was already playing. People greeted him constantly, and he gave them each a casual hello but kept steadily moving. The music enveloped the two of them as they passed through the archway.

He ditched their wineglasses and led her onto the dance floor. There, he turned her into his arms.

The silk of her dress was supple and warm. Her hand was small in his. And their thighs brushed enticingly with the rhythm of the music.

They'd barely begun, and the song ended.

"That doesn't count," he rumbled in her ear.

"Are you making up the rules?" There was a smile in her voice.

He drew back to gaze at her. "My house, my rules."

Happily, the next song was also a waltz. If he'd known he was going to meet Darci tonight, he'd have vetted the DJ's entire playlist.

"You're an autocrat?" she asked.

"Rarely."

She settled back into his arms, smoothly following his lead. "At Colborn Aerospace. Are you in charge of everything?"

"Technically, yes."

"Are you a tyrannical boss?"

He couldn't help but smile at that. "I'd say no. But probably every tyrannical boss in the world would tell you no, so you'll have to ask my staff."

Her glance darted around the dance floor. "Are any of them here?"

"A few of the senior managers. You want me to introduce you?"

"No." Her answer was quick and decisive.

"You don't want to ask them about me?"

"I don't care that much."

"Okay."

"I'm making up my own mind."

He wanted that, he realized. He really wanted this woman to have a chance to make up her own mind about him. He found himself gathering her closer.

She resisted at first, going stiff in his arms.

But he persisted, and she eventually relaxed again. Her body softened against his, her curves molding to his angles. He drew their joined hands in close to their bodies, shifting his other palm higher, to the bare skin of her back. Their movements synced, and he couldn't seem to keep his mind from wandering to a happy conclusion.

He wanted Darci Lake, wanted her very badly. He brought his cheek to her hair, inhaling a subtle scent of citrus. Her breasts had come up against his chest. Their thighs were touching, shifting together with every beat.

He gave in to temptation and kissed her hairline, whispering close to her ear. "I want you to stay tonight."

She drew back in a shot, her striking green eyes blinking. She looked truly horrified, and he could have kicked himself.

Three

Shane's proposition was a dose of reality.

Darci realized she had truly lost her mind. Her common sense had fled while she was plastered shamelessly against him, swaying to the music. No wonder he thought she was coming on to him.

His expression faltered. "I'm sorry. That didn't come out right."

But she was pretty sure it had come out exactly the way he'd meant it. And she was pretty sure she was the one to blame for leading him on.

"I meant for the rest of the party," he said. "I don't want you to leave before the end of the party."

She took a half step back, telling herself she was here to spy on Shane Colborn, not to hook up with him. Even though hooking up with him seemed like a perfectly reasonable idea.

Okay, that had to be the wine talking.

He closed the space between them. "Please don't stop dancing."

She had to own up to her part in this. "I didn't mean to give you the wrong idea."

He took her hand. "You didn't."

"We've only just met. I'm not... That is..."

He eased her into his arms, and she couldn't bring herself to fight him.

"My bad," he murmured, taking up the rhythm of the song.

She told herself to end the encounter and politely leave. She needed to regroup.

During a few bars of the music, she gathered her thoughts and then forced herself to speak. "Thank you for the tour of the wine cellar. I'm grateful that you took the time."

There was a smile in his voice, and it broke the tension. "But not that grateful?"

His unexpected joke was disarming.

"I'm never *that* grateful," she said.

"I'm very glad to hear it."

"I'm not buying that you're glad."

He chuckled. "Let's say I'm glad you've never been that grateful with any other guy."

"You have an opinion on my personal life?"

"I do."

"You do recall we met only two hours ago?"

He was silent for a moment, guiding them around the other couples on the crowded dance floor. "It seems like longer."

"Are you bored?"

"Not even a little bit." He drew back to gaze at her. "But I'm feeling oddly proprietary."

She knew she had to change the direction of the conversation, but her curiosity won out over good sense. "In what way?"

He glanced around the big room. "I don't want anyone else to dance with you."

"I doubt they will." She didn't know anyone else here.

"I'm certain they will. That is, if I let you go." He gathered her a little closer. "So, I'm not going to let you go."

That truly shouldn't sound like such a good idea.

"I don't think that's practical," she said. "You're the host."

He gave a shrug. "My cousin is helping with hosting duties."

"Isn't she busy in the wine cellar?"

"We have a caterer and fantastic staff."

"So, you plan to ignore everyone else and dance with me all night long?" As soon as the words were out, she knew she should have said evening instead of night.

His blue eyes glowed, and his voice went gravelly. "I'll do anything you want all night long."

She gave him a jab in the ribs with her elbow. "You know what I meant."

"Doesn't mean I can't tease you."

"Are you always like this?"

"Like what?"

The song changed, but she pretended not to notice. "So friendly and familiar with people you've just met?"

"Are you?"

The question took her aback. He made a good point. She was just as guilty as he was.

"I'm not," she said. "Never. That's why I assumed it had to be you."

"I'm really quite aloof."

"Sure you are."

"Ask anybody."

"I will."

"Ask Tuck."

"I am going to ask Tuck."

It was a lie. She didn't expect to ever see Tuck again.

Shane went silent for so long that she began to worry.

But then he spoke. "You never dated Tuck, did you?"

Her worry fled, and she sputtered out a laugh of surprise. "I've definitely never dated Tuck."

She realized now would be the time to confess that she didn't even know Tuck.

"Because that would be awkward," said Shane. "Tuck and I are very good friends."

Darci didn't know how to react to the statement.

"And you can't," Shane continued. "You know, with your best friend's ex. I mean, it's not a 100 percent rule, but it's kind of ironclad."

"Two hours," Darci felt compelled to point out. "Do I need to remind you again that we've only just met? We're not dating."

"We should be dating."

"You're out of your mind." She could assume only that this was some kind of well-practiced, pickup strategy.

He was pretty good at it, but she wasn't going to let herself take him seriously.

"What are you doing on Friday?" he asked.

"I'm working."

"You know I meant Friday night."

"I'm working then, too. I have my own business, and it's very busy right now."

She also had a secret job at his company, a mystery to solve and a huge vendetta against his family. He might be handsome and charming, but going on a date with Shane was out of the question.

"Give yourself some time off," he said.

"I have clients and deadlines." There was no way in the world he was talking her into a date.

"We could do dinner or take in a play. Or both. You like comedy? *The Twist* is getting rave reviews, and there's a great little seafood place about a mile from the theatre. Very posh, very exclusive."

She tipped her head back. "You do understand that I'm saying no?"

"You do understand that I'm not giving up?"

"I won't go on a date with you, Shane."

"Do you have a boyfriend?"

"No." Then she mentally kicked herself. A boyfriend would have been the perfect excuse not to see Shane again.

"Something a little more active?" he asked. "The park? The jazz festival? Or, wait, a harbor cruise?"

"Shane, stop."

"Or we could have a date right here," he carried on without stopping for a breath. "The gardens are gorgeous on a summer night. We could dine out on the deck, pick ourselves a fine bottle of wine from the cellar, now that you know what you like."

As he spoke, Darci's brain locked on to an idea. If she came back to the Colborn mansion, especially if they went down to the wine cellar, she might have another chance to snoop around. Getting to know Shane on any level was a big risk. But she'd never get back into the mansion without getting to know him at least a bit better.

A male voice interrupted them. "Why are you hogging Darci?"

Shane stiffened against her. "Hello, Tuck."

Darci twisted her head to see Tuck, shocked that he'd remembered her.

"I'm cutting in," said Tuck.

"No, you're not."

"Of course I am."

Shane looked to Darci, eyes narrowing. "I thought you said you'd never dated him."

"I haven't," she managed in a strangled voice, feeling the walls close in around her.

Something bad was about to happen.

"Quit messing around," said Tuck. "Petra's hot on my trail. I need a dance partner."

"Find another one."

"What is your *problem*?" asked Tuck.

"If you were interested in Darci, you should have said so before now."

Darci jumped in. "Listen, I—"

"Before now?" asked Tuck in clear astonishment. "When, before now?"

"I don't know," Shane drawled. "In the months, maybe the years since you met her."

If the floor would only open up and swallow her, maybe she could get herself out of this.

"Shane?" came a new female voice.

Shane turned his head.

"Looks like Maddie needs you," said Tuck.

Then he deftly tugged Darci from Shane's arms and twirled her away.

She scrambled to get her feet sorted out beneath her, regretful to leave Shane and also realizing she'd just blown her opportunity to return to the mansion. She should have accepted his invitation as soon as he'd offered it.

"Sorry about that," said Tuck, as they settled a little awkwardly into dancing. "But Petra's one determined woman."

"You seem like a very determined man."

Tuck laughed. "So was Shane. By the way, why did he think I might be dating you?"

Darci's face heated with embarrassment. "That was my fault. I'd mentioned you earlier, and he misunderstood. I should have corrected his assumption."

"Nah. It'll be more fun this way. I'd rather mess with his head. He spent most of our teenage years messing with mine."

"He did?" She was intrigued.

"We were both rich young men with fast cars, who could tip our way into the best nightclubs, but he was better looking."

"There's nothing wrong with your looks."

Tuck had heavier features than Shane, a slightly crooked smile and a scar on his chin. But he was still a handsome man.

He chuckled. "I wasn't fishing. Every time I found a new girl, Shane would flirt with her."

"That's not nice."

"He grew out of it. And, I figured out he was testing them, checking to see if they truly liked me or if they'd go with any rich guy."

"Did they all pick Shane?" She felt a rush of sympathy for Tuck.

"All except Roberta Wilson back in high school. She didn't give him a second look."

"And?" Darci prompted.

"And I dated her for six months in senior year." He shrugged. "And then it ended. She went off to a different college. Our whole carefree lifestyle ended abruptly when Shane lost his parents."

Darci was reminded that Shane hadn't always had things easy.

They danced in silence.

"It sounds like Shane is protective," said Darci, wondering how far he'd go to defend his father's honor.

"And loyal," said Tuck, then he glanced over her shoulder in Shane's direction. "So tell me about Darci Lake. I have a feeling I'll get quizzed after you leave."

Darci wasn't crazy about perpetuating a ruse with Tuck, since he was an innocent bystander. Then again, what were a few more lies? She was already in deep, and it looked as if it was going to get much deeper before it was all over.

"What do you want to know?" she asked.

"Where are you from? What do you do?"

"I grew up in Chicago, went to Columbia."

"Nice."

"I have a graphic-art business. We mostly design websites."

"That's a growth industry," said Tuck.

"So far, business is good." In fact, it was so good, between working at Colborn Aerospace during the day and trying to keep up with her website contracts at night, she was barely getting any sleep.

"I might want to hire you."

"I've got a waiting list right now." She could fit in another client, but she was staying well away from Shane's friends. "Tell me something more about you."

"Good idea. Shane will probably quiz you, too."

Darci doubted it. Once again, she mentally berated herself for having let the opportunity to come back to the mansion slip past.

"I'm the second son of Jamison Tucker, who was the only child of Randal Tucker, founder of Tucker Transportation. I'm a vice president. My older brother Dixon is the president-in-waiting."

"Does that bother you?" Darci couldn't help but ask.

"That he'll be top dog and not me? Nah. More time for me to goof off."

"Because being second in command is such an easy job?"

"It is if you—"

"You're done." Shane reappeared, scowling at Tuck.

"Looks like I'm done," Tuck agreed, letting her go. "Thank you for the dance, Darci."

"Thank you," she replied, surprised that Shane had come back to her.

He pulled her rather forcefully into his arms.

She immediately felt the difference in his posture. He was stiff, his movements jerky.

"Was that fun?" he asked her in a tight voice.

"It was fine." She struggled to find the rhythm.

"You like Tuck?"

"Tuck's perfectly nice."

"Nice?"

"Nice." The circumstances suddenly struck her as ridiculous, and she fought a grin. "Stop doing that."

"Doing what?"

"Acting like I betrayed you by dancing with Tuck. You can't lay claim to every woman you've known for two hours."

"Three hours."

"I stand corrected."

He went silent, but his movements gradually smoothed out and his shoulders seemed to relax. As the minutes ticked by, he drew her nearer, once again bringing his cheek to rest against her hair.

"Friday night?" he asked.

She saw no benefit in being coy. "On your deck? With another fine bottle of wine?"

"Absolutely."

"Then okay. It's a date."

His tone was a deep, sexy rumble. "It's a date."

She swallowed. Her stomach flip-flopped with trepidation, but she knew she had to see this through.

"Run that past me one more time," said Jennifer.

"It's the best, probably the only way to get back into his house," said Darci from the third rung of the stepladder, as she tapped a picture hook into the wall. She had no intention of repeating the details of her dance with Shane.

"So, you're dating Shane Colborn."

"I'm *pretending* to date him."

"But, he won't know you're pretending."

The hook seemed solid, so Darci went backward down the ladder. "That would be the entire point of pretending. You think the orchids on this wall or the sky scape?"

"The orchids. But you're attracted to him?"

Darci moved to the breakfast bar to retrieve a measuring tape and level. The five connected, abstract orchid paintings needed to be hung with precision.

"He's easy to be attracted to," she said.

Jennifer began tearing the brown packing paper off the largest of the orchid paintings. "And you don't think that's dangerous?"

"I'm saying I think I can pull it off without anything personal getting in the way."

He'd likely kiss her. In fact, she was positive he'd kiss her. And that was fine. What was a kiss? She could handle a kiss.

"And if you can't?" Jennifer asked.

Darci took a measure and positioned the level on the wall.

"If you've got a better idea," she said, "I'm all ears."

"You've checked the entire Colborn records center?"

"I'm still working through the stacks. I haven't found anything that old in the computer system. But there are a lot of files on paper only. It's going to take some time."

"Maybe you should finish with the office first. It seems a lot safer."

Darci made a mark with her pencil and reeled in the tape measure. "I'm doing it concurrently. I can't spend the rest of my life at this."

She needed to find her father's schematic drawings, restore his reputation as an engineer, get justice for him and quit her job at Colborn.

"I suppose." Jennifer sounded dubious.

"What exactly are you worried about?"

"That you'll get caught, of course."

Darci climbed back up the ladder, hammer and hook in hand. She had to admit, getting caught was a definite risk. She wasn't an experienced spy or a cat burglar or a con artist. This playacting and clandestine snooping was definitely out of her comfort zone.

"I don't think it's a really serious crime." She hammered as she spoke. "It's not like I'm taking anything valuable. I'll even give it all back, once I've proved my point."

Jennifer spoke over the sound of tearing paper. "If you're right, those drawings could net you millions and millions of dollars."

Darci countered, "It's not about the money."

"Maybe not to you. But it's definitely going to be about the money to Shane Colborn. All the money he stands to lose. What do you think a man like that would do to protect millions of dollars?"

Darci gave a laugh and went back to work. "You think he'll lock me in the tower or hire a hit man?"

"Hit men have been hired over a lot less."

"You've been watching too many crime dramas. Quit worrying. Now, tell me you didn't call Ashton today."

"I didn't call Ashton today." But there was a thread of guilt in Jennifer's tone.

This time Darci turned more slowly, gazing incredulously at Jennifer, who was balancing a painting against her legs. "You're lying."

"I didn't talk to him. I swear."

"But you tried," Darci guessed. "You tried, but you didn't get through?"

Jennifer glanced guiltily down. "I got his voice mail."

Darci groaned. "Please tell me you didn't leave a message."

"I didn't leave a message." Again, there was a distinct thread of guilt in Jennifer's tone.

"But?"

"I might have breathed for about five seconds. But I made the right choice. I hung up. I didn't say anything."

"He'll see your number."

"It's blocked. I blocked it."

"So that you could call Ashton?"

Jennifer tapped her fingertips along the top edge of the painting. "Maybe."

"We need to get you into a twelve-step program."

"Big talk from a woman embarking on a life of crime."

"My life of crime will have a net positive outcome. You calling Ashton is only going to mess up your life."

"I wish I could say you were wrong." Jennifer lifted the painting, then stepped forward to hand it up to Darci. "It's not that I can't see the danger. But he's like chocolate-ribbon cookie dough. You know you'll regret it in the end, but sometimes a girl just has to go for it."

"You're making me hungry."

Jennifer grinned while Darci turned to position the center painting.

"How's that?" Darci asked.

Jennifer took a few steps back. "Perfect."

She retrieved the next largest painting and passed it to Darci.

Darci married the hook to the hanger. Then she stepped down to see how they looked.

"The spacing looks right to me," said Jennifer.

There was about four inches of cream-colored wall between the two connected oils.

"You've given me a craving for ice cream," said Darci.

"We don't have any ice cream. But I do have a box of almond-caramel crunch."

"Bring it on."

While Jennifer went for the chocolates, Darci moved the ladder and measured for the next picture hook.

"Tell me about your upcoming date," Jennifer called from the kitchen.

"Dinner and wine on his deck. My plan so far is to get him to the wine cellar, pretend I need the restroom, then snoop my way through the basement."

"And if he comes after you?"

"I'll pretend I'm lost."

"It might work," Jennifer conceded.

On her return, she picked up the remote control and put on the TV in the living area. A news reporter's voice filled the background.

"He might get suspicious." Darci hung picture number three, then stepped back, liking how it looked. "But he's never going to guess the truth."

"Maybe he'll think you're a reporter writing an expose on him," said Jennifer.

"You think?" That hadn't occurred to Darci.

"You wouldn't be the first."

"What do you mean?"

"Look," said Jennifer.

Darci turned.

Jennifer pointed to the television. "Bianca Covington just published a book."

"Who's Bianca Covington?"

"Somebody gorgeous and famous, I guess."

Darci moved for a better view. A young blonde woman sat across the table from Berkley Nash, an infamous, local reporter. The camera zoomed in on a book with a fuchsia cover, titled *Shane Colborn—Behind the Mask*.

"The perils of being rich," said Jennifer.

"I wonder if it's flattering," said Darci while a headshot of Shane came up on the screen. Her chest contracted at the sight. He was cover-model gorgeous.

Suddenly, she couldn't combat her rising trepidation. Why had he been so insistent about arranging a date with her when he could have any woman in the city? Sure, she'd been wearing a four-thousand-dollar dress, and her hair and makeup had been stellar. But she was no Bianca Covington.

She had to allow for the possibility that Shane knew who she was and was stringing her along.

"There are some scandalous accusations between these pages," said Berkley.

Bianca gave a throaty laugh. "I think readers will be shocked to discover the dark side of Shane Colborn."

Jennifer raised her brows at Darci. "Dark side?"

"I'm sure she's exaggerating for ratings."

"You're going to his mansion."

"It'll be fine."

"Alone."

"He's not Count Dracula." Darci wasn't fearful at all. Well, except for the worry he might know her real identity.

"But you're going to cross him."

"I am."

"And he's got a dark side."

"Well, I have a dark side, too. I'm spying on the man."

"Ruthless," Bianca stated with conviction, her darkly outlined eyes wide. "And completely narcissistic. The silver spoon is still lodged in that man's mouth."

"That doesn't sound too bad," said Darci.

Except for the ruthless part, she supposed.

Maybe she should pick up a copy of Bianca's book before Friday, just so she'd know what she was up against.

At a corner table in Daelan's Bar and Grill, Shane could feel the critical glances of the other patrons flick from the television above the bar to him and then back again.

"It's about what we expected," said Justin as the news program moved on from Bianca. "And at least we're still in the running for the Gobrecht Airlines contract."

"She's pretty hot," said Tuck, taking a drink from the mug of lager in his hand.

Shane had a deluxe burger and fries on a plate in front of him. A minute ago, he'd been starving. But now he'd lost his appetite.

"This is going to go on for a while," he stated to no one in particular.

"She does seem to enjoy the limelight," said Justin.

"Was she worth it?" asked Tuck.

"Not even close," said Shane.

Bianca had been bubbly, energetic and fun. Agreeable to anything Shane suggested, he realized now that she'd been humoring him. She probably wasn't even a Bulls fan.

"There has to be a way to fight back," he said.

Over the past few days, he'd concluded that Justin was right. It didn't much matter what she said about their sex life. But her accusations of corporate misconduct stood to hurt Colborn Aerospace.

"Fuel to the fire," said Justin.

"Libel? Slander?" asked Shane.

"You have to be ready to prove it."

Tuck stepped in. "I'd be willing to go undercover. Date her. Sleep with her. Write some juicy lies about her."

"She knows we're friends," said Shane. Not that he'd ever agree. He wanted to stop her, not get revenge.

"Worth a try," said Tuck.

"You can't sleep with your friend's ex," said Justin.

"I *shouldn't* sleep with my friend's ex," said Tuck. "But once she betrays him, all bets are off. Shane doesn't care if I sleep with her. Do you, Shane?"

"The woman can sleep with an entire offensive line for all I care."

"See?" said Tuck.

"You have no morals," said Justin.

"Bianca has no morals," said Shane.

Tuck raised his glass. "I think we can all agree on that."

The men clicked mugs, and each took a swig of beer.

"So, what happened with Darci?" asked Tuck.

"You stay away from Darci," Shane warned, deciding to eat some of the fries, after all. No point in starving for the sake of his deceitful, immoral ex.

"Who's Darci?" asked Justin.

"The anti-Bianca," said Shane.

"She saves orphans and feeds the hungry?"

"It was all I could do to get her to say yes to a date with me."

"Date?" Justin's attention immediately perked up. "What date?"

"She could be purposely playing hard to get," said Tuck.

"Not my take," Shane said to Tuck, ignoring Justin. "But you know her. What's she like?"

"Grew up in Chicago," said Tuck. "She went to Colombia. From what I can tell, she's a regular gal. Has her own business, designing websites."

"You need to stay stag for a while," said Justin.

"Relax. It's dinner at the mansion. No crowds, no cameras, just the two of us."

Something warm settled inside Shane when he thought about Friday's date. Darci seemed so fresh and genuine. That she'd chosen the privacy of his mansion over a play and a trendy restaurant was a good sign. She reminded him that not all women fixated on his wealth and status. Sometimes, they simply wanted to get to know him.

Four

"You read the book?" Shane asked as he topped up Darci's wineglass and then refilled his own.

"Of course I read the book," she answered.

Finally, they'd emptied the bottle of wine that had been open and on the table when they started dinner. Maybe now she had a chance at getting to the wine cellar.

"I'm sorry you did that," he said.

"Because it's unflattering?"

"Because it's unflattering, and it's nowhere near to being true."

She didn't blame him for being upset about the book. True or not, she sure wouldn't want people to read such intimate details about her.

"Tell me which parts are lies."

"It would be a lot faster to tell you which parts were true."

Candlelight flickered in the warm night breeze. The scent of roses wafted up from the gardens while leaves rustled in the oak trees beneath a panorama of stars.

"Okay. Which parts are true?" She raised her glass to her lips. She was already feeling a bit lightheaded, but she couldn't suggest they head down to the wine cellar until she polished off this last glass.

"My name *is* Shane Colborn."

She waited.

Then she smiled at what she assumed was his joke. "Yeah, I'm not buying that."

"That my name is Shane Colborn? I have government-issued ID to prove it."

"Own it, Shane. What else is true?"

He twirled the stem of his wineglass. "She got my car right, make and model, not the year. We did spend a weekend in Aspen. But her tour of the Colborn facility stopped at the executive boardroom and my private—" He paused to take a sip of his wine.

She struggled not to snicker at his obvious embarrassment.

He frowned at her. "We never even went *near* my private bathroom, never mind had sex in it."

"I'm not judging."

He drew a breath. "I sure never discussed clients with her and never anything about a business deal. I wouldn't do that. She wouldn't have understood anyway."

"So, how'd it get in the book?"

"Some of the information was on the public record, and some was fabricated. She must have had an expert do research for her to give it an air of authenticity."

Darci kept her expression neutral. "And they discovered you were stealing intellectual property?"

"That part was *entirely* a lie. I'm saying she found someone to help her make the lie sound credible."

"That seems like a lot of work." Darci couldn't help but wonder if Shane had inherited his father's deceitful inclinations.

Shane's eyes narrowed, and she quickly realized she had to do a better job of acting. Now wasn't the time to accuse him of anything dishonest, no matter how emotionally satisfying it might feel in the moment.

"I meant she doesn't strike me as the type to undertake complicated research and analysis to reach her goal," said Darci.

"You got that right," said Shane. "Somebody else might be pulling the strings. On the surface, it looks like a vindictive ex-girlfriend out for monetary gain. But it could be someone using her to go after me and Colborn Aerospace. We're in the midst of some delicate contract negotiations. It could be a competitor."

"Is that what you think?" The complexity of his theory told Darci that Shane was familiar with underhanded corporate schemes. Probably because he undertook them himself.

"It has to be one or the other," he said.

"I suppose."

"What's your theory?"

"I don't have a theory."

"Come up with one."

She thought about it. "Maybe you're lying, and everything she says is true."

He didn't miss a beat. "You could come to bed with me and find out."

"That wasn't the part—" She'd meant the corporate stories, not the lovemaking stories. "You're joking." Of course he was joking.

A gleam came into his blue eyes. "Would you like it if I waxed poetic?"

She gave him a mock minitoast that reminded her to keep drinking. "Nice try, but I'm not walking into that one."

"I've never quoted Byron before, but I'm willing to give it a shot."

She polished off her wine. Then she gave him what she hoped was an enigmatic smile. "Any chance of getting ourselves another bottle?"

"I'll have one brought up."

"I'd rather go down and browse."

He looked confused. "That's not necessary. We don't need to—"

"It was fun last time. And I was hoping to learn a little more about wine."

His expression softened. "Okay then. Whatever you'd like." He rose, moved around the table and pulled back her chair.

"This is very accommodating of you," she said.

"Despite what Bianca's telling the world, I'm a perfectly wonderful guy."

Darci set her linen napkin on the table and came to her feet. "I'll admit you have a great wine cellar. And your manners are faultless and the place is stunning. That's all very classy."

"That's just the money," he said, a slight edge to his voice as they crossed to the open patio doors.

"You do have a lot of money."

"Sometimes it's annoying."

She didn't believe that for a minute. "You're saying you'd rather people liked you for who you are?"

"Wouldn't everybody like that?"

"Then why serve me dinner in a mansion with, I don't know, two dozen staff members?"

He hesitated. "Because you said yes."

He had a point there.

"Also to impress you," he said.

"I don't think you can have it both ways."

"Usually, I can."

"Until Bianca came along?"

"I'm tired of talking about Bianca."

"Sorry." Darci could have kicked herself.

"She was *only* ever interested in the money. And now I want it the other way. I want to meet someone who doesn't care about the money."

"It'll be tricky to find a woman who doesn't know about your wealth. You were famous before, doubly now."

They made it to the top of the basement stairs.

"Do you think that many people will read the book?" he asked.

She was pretty sure they would. "It had its very own display, right up at the front of the store."

Shane swore under his breath, and for a second, she actually felt sorry for him.

"That's probably just in Chicago," she said.

His voice took on a note of horror. "You think it's like that all over Chicago?"

She thought maybe the entire Midwest, but she didn't say so.

"There's something fundamentally wrong," he said as he led the way down the staircase, "when a person can say or do anything that destroys another person's reputation, no matter how outrageous or untrue, and there's virtually no defense."

Darci's tone went flat. "No kidding."

She couldn't help but wonder if Shane knew about his father's treachery, how Dalton Colborn had ruined her own father's reputation and life. On the scale of things, Shane's family was far worse than Bianca.

They turned and walked down the hallway to the large wooden door of the wine cellar. There, he crouched down and slid open a discreet panel at the bottom corner and extracted the key.

"Now you know the secret," he said as he inserted it into the lock.

She forced away her anger, cautioning herself to keep her emotions under control. "I thought you carried the key with you."

"I just took it out for the party. Can't have a dozen guests know where to find it."

"I'm honored that you—" She stopped herself, swallowing the words *trust me.*

She pushed down a surge of guilt. She absolutely shouldn't be trusted.

"Here we go," he said.

The door opened inward, and he flipped on the lights.

Darci found herself amazed all over again at the size of the cellar and at the sheer number of bottles stacked in the racks.

"How do you navigate your way through all this?" she found herself asking with genuine curiosity.

"It's organized by continent and country," he answered, walking toward the back. "Then by region and grape variety. And there's a general bottom-to-top price trend."

She tipped her head to one side. "The really good stuff is up high?"

"The taller you are, the better in here."

She smiled. "I'd need a ladder."

"There's a rickety step stool in the corner. The theory being, if you're too drunk to climb up to the good stuff, you're too drunk to appreciate it." He took a couple of paces. "Here we are in the Bordeaux region of France."

"Old World?" she guessed.

"This section will be mostly cabernet sauvignon grapes. If

we move to the left, there'll be more merlot in the blend. Did you like the bottle we just had?"

"It was fantastic." She feared she was getting spoiled.

"Then maybe…" He stretched to reach up.

"Still trying to impress me?" she asked.

"How am I doing so far?"

He turned to gaze at her with a warm smile, and her breath caught in her throat. His lips were full, his expression soft. A sensual glow lurked deep in his eyes. He was tall, strong, handsome and sexy. He was also smart, classy and funny.

If she hadn't been spying on him, hadn't known the dark secret of his family's wealth, she probably would have thrown herself into his arms. Instead, she ruthlessly reminded herself of her mission.

"Is there a washroom down here?" she forced herself to ask.

"That's a cop-out."

It certainly was. "When I stood up, I realized…"

"Back the way we came. Want me to show you?"

"No, no. I'm sure I'll be fine."

"It's the door just past the staircase."

"Thanks."

"No problem. I'll find us something great while you're gone."

She nodded as she backed away.

"Watch—"

She banged her hip on a chair.

"—out for the table," he finished.

"Ouch."

"You okay?"

"Just clumsy." She turned and headed out the door.

As soon as she was out of sight, she picked up her pace, stopping to crack open each door along the way and take a look inside. She found a pantry, furniture storage and exercise equipment. A hallway branched off to the right, but she didn't have time to explore it.

The basement was far too big to investigate in five minutes. It was going to take more than a single trip down here, which probably meant more than one date. Which in turn meant she'd have to get Shane to invite her back.

She'd have to pretend she was romantically interested in him. She'd have to kiss him, maybe even a little more. A shiver ran up her spine at the thought. She hoped it was revulsion, but she feared it was excitement.

Telling herself to get a grip, she stopped in front of another door and reached for the handle.

Frantic barking startled Shane, and he nearly dropped the bottle of 1990 Chateau Cauchon.

He rushed from the cellar into the hall, his thoughts immediately going to Darci.

"Gus," he shouted down the passageway. "Boomer, off!"

The barking immediately stopped.

"Sit," Shane called, pacing down the hall.

Darci was plastered against the wall, both black Newfoundlands sitting directly in front of her. As he grew closer, he could see she looked terrified.

"They won't hurt you," he assured her. "Gus, Boomer, come here."

They both immediately came to their feet and trotted down the hall.

"Lie down," he commanded. "Stay."

Then he quickly went to Darci. "How did they get—?" He noticed the yard door standing open. He turned his attention to her, puzzled. "Why did you let the dogs in?"

"I…" She swallowed. She was white as a sheet.

"Hey." He reflexively drew her into his arms. "It's okay. I'm sorry if they scared you."

"I picked the wrong door," she said against his shoulder. "They just barreled right inside."

"I bet they did."

Her body was warm against his. He knew he shouldn't notice the curve of her thighs and the softness of her breasts, but he couldn't help himself. She smelled like wildflowers, and his arms tightened instinctively around her.

"They're big," she said. "And they're loud."

"They're perfectly friendly, as long as you're not stealing anything."

Her breathing stopped.

He drew away to look at her. "What's wrong?"

She pushed back her hair. When she spoke, there was a slight tremor in her voice. "They don't know me. They could have easily mistaken me for a burglar."

"Let's go introduce you."

"No!"

He took in her wide eyes and her pale complexion. "Are you afraid of dogs?"

It took her a moment to speak. "Kind of. Okay, yes. More the big ones. And those two are *huge*."

"Newfoundlands are gentle and affectionate."

She slanted a gaze down the hall, looking decidedly suspicious.

"Darci?"

"Yes?"

"I now feel obligated to cure you."

"You're not going to cure me."

"Why not?"

"I've been this way my whole life."

"What happened?"

"Nothing."

"It's never nothing. Humans are naturally drawn to animals. If you're afraid of them, it's for a reason."

She pressed her lips tight together.

"Tell me," he said.

"It's embarrassing." She seemed to suddenly realize she was in his arms, and she shifted away.

He reluctantly let her go. "Were you bitten?"

"No."

He was glad to hear that. "Chased?"

She glared at him.

"If I ply you with a little more wine, are you likely to tell me?"

There was another silence.

He waited.

She cracked first. "It was a dream, okay?"

"You dreamed about vicious dogs?"

She nodded. "When I was a kid, there was this black mastiff that was penned up behind our apartment block. It was probably four times my size. The kids all played out in the back, and I was always afraid it would jump the fence and get me."

"Did you tell anyone you were scared?"

"No. None of the other kids seemed to care. It was just me, so I kept my mouth shut and pretended I was brave, too."

"And it gave you nightmares?"

"All the time. Can we drink wine now?"

He couldn't hold back a smile. "We have to pass the dogs to get to the glasses."

She went still again.

"I'll protect you."

"Do I have to pass them to get to the washroom?"

He gave her a questioning look.

"I can probably forgo a wineglass, but I definitely can't skip the washroom."

"You should meet the dogs. You'll like them, I promise." Then he gestured with his free hand. "Washroom's in there. Me and the dogs will wait."

"You're just plain mean."

"It's for your own good, Darci."

"I didn't come here for my own good." Her words were bold, but unease flitted through her eyes, giving her an aura of vulnerability.

Compassion unexpectedly welled up inside him. He reached up to touch her cheek. "I'm glad you came. I'm not going to push you. I'll put the dogs back outside."

She filled her lungs, looking as if she was trying to muster her courage.

"It's okay. I'll meet them."

"No need. I shouldn't have pressed." He wasn't her psychologist, and he sure didn't want to make things worse.

"You'll protect me?"

Something tightened inside his chest. "I promise."

She looked suddenly delicate in the slim-cut, green-and-gold dress. The shimmering fabric accentuated her stunning figure. The colors reflected her eyes, and the scooped neckline only hinted at the cleavage below. Her shoulders were smooth beneath narrow straps. A pulse beat at the base of her slender neck.

The urge to run his fingertips across her skin was overpowering. The urge to kiss her mouth was stronger still. He fought it for a long minute.

But then, very slowly, with infinite care, he reached up to cup her cheek. Her irises deepened to moss green, her pupils dilating with a blink of her long lashes.

Desire steamed inside him, urging him onward.

With a tight breath, he gave in. He dipped his head, putting his lips softly to hers.

Her kiss was hesitant, but she was definitely kissing him back. Her lips were delectable.

He closed the space between them, slipping his forearm across the small of her back, bringing her against him. He cursed the bottle of wine in his hand, which compromised the embrace.

He broke the kiss for a split second, just long enough to reposition. She tipped her head to the side, opening to him. Their kiss lengthened and deepened.

Her arms slid around his neck. He moved, backing her to the wall, bringing their bodies satisfyingly tight together, pressing his thigh to the seam of hers.

His tongue swooped in, and hers parried. His fingers spread, delving into the rich mane of her hair. He could feel his control leech away. He wanted far more than she could possibly want to give. For a moment, he rode the wave, his imagination taking flight and his body ramping up for fulfillment.

At the brink, he dragged himself back. He had to stop. He wouldn't make the same mistake as last weekend and frighten her off.

He eased his fingers from her hair, drew slowly away from her lips and released the pressure of his forearm on her back.

He took a couple of careful breaths, willing his hormones to settle.

Her green eyes were luminous, cheeks flushed, lips bright red and excruciatingly kissable. Her sweet breath puffed against his face, and he didn't think he could step away.

"Washroom's through that door," he managed in a low tone, canting his head.

It took her a beat to respond. Her voice was breathy as she eased back. "Yes. Right."

It was satisfying to know the kiss had rattled her, too.

"You want me to put the dogs outside?"

"Sure. No. I don't know."

He couldn't resist smoothing her tousled hair. "They're really very sweet."

Her hand went to her stomach. "I'm scared."

"That's understandable." He waited.

"Okay," she said. "I'll do it."

"Good girl."

She stepped away, gaze still locked with his. She took a few backward paces before she turned into the washroom and closed the door.

Shane staggered backward, leaning against the opposite wall for support. That was hands-down the most incredible kiss of his life. He was stunned by the strength of his desire. She was sexy and gorgeous. But she was also smart, determined and funny, and now he knew she was emotional and vulnerable.

He desperately wanted to make love to her. But he also wanted to know her. He closed his eyes, gave his head an abrupt shake, ruthlessly tamping down his lust. He was *not* going to attempt to seduce her.

The washroom door opened, and she returned to the hall. He straightened to meet her.

"I'm ready," she told him.

His hormones sang with delight. But then his rational brain

kicked back in, and he realized she was talking about Gus and Boomer.

"The one closest to the wall is Gus," he said, diverting his own attention. "The other is Boomer."

"How can you tell them apart?"

"Gus's face is more square, and his ears are slightly shorter."

"Are you teasing me?"

"No."

"They're identical."

"Not once you get to know them. Gus is also shorter and maybe five pounds lighter."

"How much do they weigh?"

"Around a hundred and twenty or hundred and thirty."

"That's more than me."

He resisted an urge to put an arm around her again. She was absolutely the perfect size and shape for his taste. Her legs were long, her waist nipped in, hips nicely rounded, with beautifully sized breasts that he was dying to caress.

He dragged himself back to reality once again. "They're three years old. They're past the adolescent stage, so they're quite calm."

"Calm," Darci muttered under her breath.

"First thing you want to do is let them sniff the back of your hand."

"Will they bite?"

"*No.* They're not going to bite you. I'd never put you anywhere near a dog that might bite you."

"Okay." But she sounded skeptical.

"They'll sniff your hand. Then you can pat them on the head. Then we'll drink some wine."

"That's it?"

"That's it." He held up the bottle that was still in his hand. "And this is from the top shelf. Think of it as a reward."

She managed a small smile. "You're going for the positive-reinforcement method?"

"Pat a dog. Get a glass of Chateau Cauchon. I doubt it's been tried before, but I bet it works."

Her steps slowed.

"You can do it," he told her.

She squared her shoulders.

Both dogs sat up eagerly on their haunches as he and Darci approached.

"Stay," Shane warned.

"You mean them, right?" said Darci.

"You're funny."

"I'm terrified."

"You're still funny. Now hold out your hand, the back side up."

She reached out, trembling slighting.

He gave in and wrapped an arm around her shoulders.

Gus leaned forward and sniffed. He wrinkled his nose and blinked up at her.

"He's huge," said Darci.

Boomer went next, nudging Gus aside.

"Scratch the top of his head," said Shane.

Darci took a moment but then reached forward.

Boomer tipped his head to one side to watch her hand.

"It's okay. He's probably more scared of you than you are of him."

"You're lying."

"True. I'm lying. He loves people. He's hoping you'll throw a ball or get down on the floor and romp with him."

Her fingers contacted his head, and she scratched.

Boomer gave slow blinks of ecstasy.

Gus nudged his way in, and Darci petted him, too.

"There you go," said Shane. "You're done."

He felt the tension flow out of her body.

"I lived," she said.

"And now you get wine."

With a brief detour through a big, modern kitchen, Shane showed Darci to a small sitting room on the second floor. She immediately liked it. In contrast to the rest of the mansion, the room was compact and cozy. The ceiling here was lower, the color tones softer, and the furniture slightly worn, with a pretty bay window looking over a small grove of oak trees.

"This is nice," she said as she sat down in a soft moss green armchair.

"It's my favorite room," said Shane, removing his suit jacket and laying it aside.

He took the companion chair and set the wine and the glasses on a small round table between them.

There were two love seats in the room, facing each other across an oversize ottoman with a wooden tray in the center. The tray held a copper bowl of nuts, two decorative candles and a tasteful floral display. Sconce lighting on the walls was yellow in tone, and a few abstract oils hung on the walls. Giant potted plants bracketed the sitting area.

Darci wanted to kick off her tight shoes and curl her legs beneath her. But she didn't want to come across as presumptuous.

He poured the wine.

Then he lifted his glass. "To your bravery."

She followed suit. "You mean my irrational fear."

"All fears are rooted in logic." He paused. "Then again, they're all somewhat irrational."

She touched her glass to his. "That's very generous."

He smiled and took a sip.

She did the same, and the smooth flavors bloomed on her tongue.

"What do you think?" he asked.

"Oh my. That is *very* nice."

With this kind of positive reinforcement, he could get her to do just about anything.

"Nineteen ninety was a good year in Bordeaux."

She took another sip. "Wow. Okay, I'm thinking about getting a puppy."

Shane laughed, but his expression turned intimate. "If only it was that easy."

Suddenly, she felt self-conscious about all she'd shared with him. "I didn't mean to throw you into the middle of my phobia."

"Don't worry about it. Every kid has nightmares and irra-tional fears. Most of us never get over them."

"Us?" Was he saying what she thought he was saying?

"I was a kid once."

She tried to picture it. "You don't seem like the fearful type."

"All kids get scared, including me."

"Well, thank goodness for that." Then she realized how she'd sounded. "I mean, that's too bad. Okay, what I really mean is spit it out, Shane."

"I like you, Darci."

That wasn't what she was going for. At least it sure wasn't what she was supposed to be going for. But his words warmed her. She desperately wished she could like him, too, especially after that incredible kiss. But she didn't dare. She couldn't af-ford to let her emotions complicate the situation.

She forced a teasing lilt to her voice. "Are you stalling?"

"I'm not. Okay, I am."

"Just say it."

"Fine." He set down his glass. "With me, it's the money."

That didn't make any sense at all. "I can't believe you're afraid of wealth."

"I'm afraid of the implications of having it. When I was about eight, I overheard a conversation between my dad and someone else—I can't even remember who—but they were talking about the potential for kidnapping and ransom."

"Kidnapping you?" Okay, that made sense.

Shane nodded. "For some reason, it really hit home. I had visions of being tied up, gagged and thrown in the trunk of a car."

Her heart went out to him. "That sounds terrifying for a little kid."

"In retrospect, I probably shouldn't have watched so many cop shows."

"Did you tell anyone?"

"Never have. Not until now."

"Thanks." She appreciated his moral support. "But yours is nowhere near a phobia."

"It still impacts my life."

"You don't walk around the city in fear of every man or car that comes along."

"True," he agreed. "But I surround myself with state-of-the-art security."

"That's just logical."

"And I'm hyperaware of the perils of wealth."

Her sympathy took a dip. "There are a lot of perils, are there?"

To her mind, the perils of this particular situation were what her father had endured—betrayal, defeat and a marginal income instead of significant income.

"It's not all caviar and mansions. Just look at the Bianca situation."

"Due respect, Shane, you're worried Chicago's finest bachelorettes will think you quote Byron between the silk sheets?"

He frowned. "I'm worried that clients will cancel multimillion-dollar contracts."

"And your enormous net worth might drop a little?"

"And," he said, tone hardening, "I worry about not knowing who's a friend and who'll betray me."

For a horrible second, Darci thought she was caught.

She braced herself for his accusation.

When he stayed silent, guilt assailed her. She swallowed against a dry throat.

She reached for the wineglass, but that made her feel worse. He was sharing this amazing bottle of wine. He'd invited her into his home, had showed her compassion and understanding while she was being completely underhanded.

To top it off, now she'd ridiculed him.

"I'm really sorry," she said in a low voice.

"You're allowed to have an opinion."

She shook her head. "That was thoughtless. I didn't mean to suggest you have no problems."

He stared at her for a very long moment. "I don't want to fight with you, Darci."

"I don't want to fight with you, either."

That was the truth. She wanted to hug him. She wanted to kiss him. She wanted to be wrapped in his strong arms all over again and never come up for air.

Oh, this was not good.

"Glad we've got that straight," he said easily.

She was anxious to move on. "Tell me about your security system."

"You want to see how my childhood fear turned into an adult phobia?" He grinned.

"I do." What she really wanted was a safe topic of conversation.

"To keep my personal nightmares at bay, I have monitored alarm systems, both here and at the penthouse. The mansion has exterior cameras, motion detectors, gas and fire and perimeter alarms, all managed by four hidden control panels."

"Wow." That *was* state-of-the-art.

"I can turn the system on or off from the entry hall, the kitchen pantry, the basement and the master bedroom." He cracked a mischievous smile and waggled his brows. "I'll show you that one anytime you like."

She struggled not to laugh. "You do know that's not going to happen."

"I do, indeed."

"I mean—"

She abruptly stopped herself. What was she going to say? Not tonight but maybe another night? Not tonight and not any night. She couldn't go anywhere near Shane's bedroom, ever. But she couldn't say that, even when the silence stretched.

He finally broke it. "We have a service that patrols the neighborhood here. And the dogs, though they're more for show than anything."

"They'd work on me," she said, struggling for composure.

"At the penthouse," he continued. "It's just the electronic system, but there's a security guard on duty in the lobby."

"I have to say, that doesn't really sound like a phobia."

"Do you have an alarm system?"

"No, we don't."

His head came up. "We?"

"I have a roommate."

"Platonic?"

"She likes to keep it that way. Her name's Jennifer."

"Okay."

"I'm not dating anyone, Shane." They'd gone through this last weekend.

"I guess I'm just a bit jumpy when it comes to relationships."

"I understand."

She didn't know what else to say. She couldn't swear she'd never lie to him. She'd already lied outright. And her lie of omission was a thing to behold.

"Would you come here?" he asked in a soft tone.

Her chest contracted. "There?"

He nodded. "I respect your no. I'm not trying to press. I just…"

A wave of longing washed through her. She recognized the danger, but she was so tempted.

His voice was deep, sexy, persuasive. "Nobody takes off their clothes and no hands below the waist."

"Can you stick to those rules?"

"I can if you can."

"I can." She had no choice.

He smiled. "Come here."

Heart thudding, she rose. Her brain screamed at her to stop, but she didn't. She took the three steps that brought her in front of him.

The air went thick between them.

He reached for her hand and drew her down, crossways onto his lap. His thighs were taut, his chest firm and broad. He smelled fresh and earthy. His arm curled around her, urging her in, settling her against his chest and shoulder.

She knew she shouldn't relax, but she couldn't help herself.

Just for a few minutes, she promised. She felt the strength and the intimacy of his body beneath hers. It was hot and sexy, and absolutely forbidden.

"This is a mistake," she said, more to herself than to him.

"No, it's not. It's the smartest thing I've ever done." He placed the gentlest of kisses at her hairline.

Her limbs softened. It was only a kiss. She could handle a kiss. They'd pledged not to take it further.

She lifted her chin, giving access to her lips.

He instantly took the invitation, bending forward. His mouth met hers, and sensation rocketed through her.

The kiss grew harder and deeper. She arched her back, and he wrapped his arms fully around her.

She slid her hands along his body, feeling the heat through his dress shirt, the hardness of his stomach, the definition of his pecs, the broad strength of his shoulders. She came to his tie and fingered the knot.

He murmured her name, his kisses moving to her neck, downward, across her shoulder, pushing aside the fabric and the strap of her bra. A shimmer started in the pit of her stomach, radiating outward, urging her on.

She kissed his neck, his earlobe, his cheek, then he met her with his mouth, sending bells clanging inside her head, colored rainbows popping up behind her eyes.

Then she realized the bells were real.

It was a phone, his phone, on the table beside them.

He swore under his breath and reached out.

It rang again.

"It's my lawyer," he said.

"Go ahead."

Her breathing was labored. Her skin tingled, and her entire body throbbed with unfulfilled desire. She had not been about to stop.

He swore again. Then he put the phone to his ear.

"Hey, Justin." Shane's voice was remarkably even.

If she hadn't been sitting in his lap, feeling every nuance

of his body, she'd have guessed their kisses hadn't affected him at all.

"Damn it." His tone was sharp.

Darci knew she had to move. She should be thankful for the interruption and get the heck up. She couldn't be trusted with Shane, and she had to leave here now.

"Paris?" He waited while Justin obviously spoke. "Yeah. Okay."

She tried to move away, but he instantly tightened his hold.

"Hang on," he said into the phone. Then he muffled it against his chest. "Don't go."

"I have to."

"No, you don't."

"Shane, we can't."

"We won't."

"We were about to."

He stared at her, jaw clenched. Then he put the phone back to his ear. "I'll call you back." He waited again. "Two minutes." He sucked in what sounded like a frustrated breath. "Yes! Just wait." He hit the end button and tossed the phone onto the table.

"I have to go," she repeated, pushing away.

This time he released her.

She came to her feet, straightened her dress. "I'm so sorry."

"Don't be sorry."

"The wine." She gestured to the expensive bottle, which they'd barely begun to drink. "We hardly—"

"Forget the wine."

She wished she could explain why she couldn't sleep with him. She wanted to sleep with him. She wanted it badly. But that was a line she couldn't cross.

"I have to go to France," he said.

"Right now?" She was sharply reminded of who he was and the life he led.

"In the morning. It's that stupid Bianca book. A German company canceled an important order, and now a French company is hesitating. I'm sorry, but—"

"Don't *you* be sorry. It's your job. I get it."

"You have to come back," he said.

"I don't know." Her stomach cramped with anxiety. She had to look further for her father's drawings, but she couldn't risk a repeat of tonight.

"Next Saturday," he said. "In the daylight. We'll do something outside with the dogs."

This was a disaster. She'd lost all perspective, and he had to think she was some lunatic, Victorian throwback.

"I wish I could explain."

"You don't have to explain." He came to his feet and picked up his phone. "Just say yes."

She had to say no. She couldn't trust herself with him. But she had to say yes, or all of this had been a waste.

"There's only one acceptable answer," he told her gently.

"Okay," she agreed. "Okay."

She'd try this one more time. But she wasn't going to let herself be alone with him, not even for a moment.

Five

It was close to midnight when Darci let herself into the quiet apartment. Jennifer had left a small light on above the kitchen counter, and the city glow shone in through the big windows.

Darci dropped her purse on a table and kicked off her shoes. The effects of the wine were starting to wear off, and her energy had leeched away. She felt like a fool. She felt weak and stupid and ridiculously vulnerable to her hormones.

A big glass of water, a quick shower and the comfort of her soft sheets was the smart course of action right now. But she wasn't having a particularly smart night. And her stomach hurt. And she had to talk this out.

So instead of heading for her own bedroom, she took the narrow staircase to Jennifer's bedroom loft.

"You awake," she stage-whispered at the top of the stairs.

Jennifer rustled in her bed. "Huh?"

"You awake?" Darci repeated, although the answer was obvious. She moved toward Jennifer's double bed, navigating by the glow from the windows.

"Sure. Yeah. I'm awake. How'd it go?" Jennifer wriggled into a sitting position against her headboard.

Darci sat down at the foot of the bed, curling her feet beneath her. "Not so good. Terrible, in fact. I didn't find anything. And…well…" She plucked at the comforter.

"What?" asked Jennifer.

"I get it now." The cramp in her stomach tightened.

"You get what?"

"I get the thing with Ashton. Knowing you can't but wanting so desperately to figure out a way that it's okay, and then throwing caution to the wind and ending up in a place where you…"

Jennifer sat up straight. "Darci, what did you *do*?"

"Not that. I didn't do that. But I thought about doing that.

I almost did that. I'm pretty sure I'd have done it if not for his lawyer."

"I know it's late. And I'm kinda fuzzy here. But what are you talking about?"

"Sex."

"I *know* you're talking about sex. But what's the context? How did you almost have it? And with *Shane Colborn*?"

"He's pretty hot," said Darci, her memory going back. "Maybe it was the wine."

"Are you drunk?"

"Not really. We only had one bottle. Well, he opened another. And I'm afraid it was really expensive. But then he kissed me, and I ended up in his lap. And, oh man, Jen, it was...oh man."

It took Jennifer a moment to speak. "You can't fall for Shane Colborn."

"You think I don't know that?"

"Maybe Ashton can't be trusted. But Shane is your enemy."

"He's not—" Darci winced. "Yes. You're right. He's the enemy."

"And you're spying on him."

"I am. I'm not doing that great a job of it. But I am trying."

"So far, I'm impressed. You got into his mansion twice. Did you get down to the basement? Did you find out anything new?"

"I found his dogs."

"Dogs?"

"Big dogs. Big loud dogs."

"Uh-oh."

"Yeah." Darci couldn't help remembering how great Shane had been about that part, too. "There wasn't nearly enough time to look around. I know some of the places where the records *aren't*, but there are so many other rooms down there."

"Maybe this isn't such a good idea."

"I'm going back next weekend."

"Going back won't solve the problem. He's not going to let you loose in his basement for hours by yourself."

Darci had to admit Jennifer was right. Even if she did find the records, she'd never have time to look through them. And she could hardly leave the mansion with an armful of file folders.

But then what? Did she simply give up? Did she let someone else claim her father's legacy forever?

Jennifer's fan oscillated in the corner while traffic hummed past on the streets below. A jet plane rumbled in the distance on its way into O'Hare.

"Could you get in while he wasn't there?" asked Jennifer.

"I don't see how. He's got this elaborate alarm system. And security. And the dogs." Darci gave a weak laugh. "I'm not a cat burglar. I'm not breaking into Shane's home, no matter how noble my cause."

"I suppose that is over-the-top," said Jennifer. "Then again, so is sleeping with him to get him to trust you."

"That wasn't why I was going to sleep with him."

"Why exactly were you going to sleep with him? We both know that with you it takes more than a buff, good-looking guy."

It was a very good question. What was it about Shane?

"Darci?" Jennifer prompted.

"I'm thinking. I don't really know. He's…nice. He's funny and smart and considerate. And he smells, well, it's hard to describe, but it's good. He picks up on everything I say. He gets it. He laughs in all the right places. And he's got this twinkle in his blue eyes, like he can see right through you, knows what's going on inside your head."

"He doesn't know you're spying on him."

"He doesn't. But every once in a while." Darci tried to put it into words. "If I slip up in even the slightest way, he gets suspicious. It's like he knows there's something more going on, but he can't quantify it, and for some reason, he doesn't want to ask."

"Maybe because he wants to get you into bed?"

"He's made no secret of that. But he's respectful of me saying no."

"Or he pretends to be respectful. It was the lawyer that shut it down, not Shane, right?"

That was true. Darci nodded. "He has to go to France."

"The lawyer?"

"Shane. First thing tomorrow. It sounded like he'd be gone a few days."

"Perfect time for a burglary."

"If I was willing to do that."

Jennifer slid forward and wrapped her arms around her knees, a sly expression coming over her face. "What if you didn't break in?"

Darci twisted to face her. "I'm not going to break in."

"What if they invited you in?"

"He will. He has."

Jennifer gave her head a shake. "When he's not there. What if the staff would let you in when he's not there?"

"Why would they do that? And, anyway, they'd tell him I'd been there."

"So you'd need a good excuse."

"Like what?" It was too bad Darci wasn't a dog person. She might have used them as a reason to go back.

"You lost something," said Jennifer. "You lost something, and you need to look for it. It has huge sentimental value, and you'll be upset until you find it."

She reached out and grasped Darci's chin, turning her head from side to side. "Those are opals."

"My earrings?"

"Yes. You can say you inherited them from your mother. No, your grandmother. Your beloved grandmother, who wore them on her wedding day. You lost one in…" Jennifer tipped back her head and laughed.

"I never met my grandmother, either of them."

"In the *wine cellar*," Jennifer chortled. "You lost an heirloom opal earring in the wine cellar, and you have to look for it. You won't sleep until it's safe in your hands."

"That's ridiculous."

"It's brilliant."

"It's a big, fat lie. And what if Shane remembers I was wearing both my earrings when I left his house."

"He's a regular guy. He doesn't remember."

"He could."

"He won't. And if he does, then you say you lost it in the apartment and only *thought* you lost it in the wine cellar."

"That's a pretty complicated lie."

"Everything you've done so far has been a pretty complicated lie, Darci *Lake*. This is a brilliant plan. It'll give you plenty of time alone in his basement."

Darci thought it through. "He did show me where they hide the key to the wine cellar."

"It's locked?"

"They have some pretty expensive wines down there." Darci felt guilty all over again, for having barely touched the second bottle.

Jennifer was grinning. "You can do this."

Darci had to admit, she could. Though it felt fundamentally wrong, it also felt fundamentally logical. She couldn't snoop properly when Shane was around. So she had to do it when he was away.

Shane frowned at Tuck from across a table in the restaurant of the Platinum Hotel in Paris. "I should have left you in Chicago and flown commercial."

"Give your head a shake," said Tuck, sprinkling salt on his scrambled eggs. "You were in a hurry. And what's the point of owning a transportation company, if I can't make use of the transportation?"

"I didn't expect the third degree."

"I only said you're slipping," said Tuck. "She seemed like a perfectly nice woman."

"I was jet-lagged last night. And I'm here to focus on business, not women."

"And I told *you*, she didn't seem like the type to still be hanging around this morning."

"And this way, she's not," said Shane.

His meeting this afternoon with Beaumont Air was vital to the financial health of Colborn Aerospace.

"That's playing it ludicrously safe," said Tuck, his hand moving to the small pitcher of maple syrup.

"This way, I'm focused." Shane didn't care to admit that the beautiful leggy brunette who'd approached their table in the lounge last night hadn't interested him in the least. His tastes ran to Darci right now, and nobody else seemed to measure up.

"You're distracted."

"Yes." That much was true. "By the Beaumont meeting."

Tuck shook his head. "I'm not talking about business. I'm still talking about women. So, is it Darci Lake?"

Shane's guard went up. "What makes you ask that?"

"Are you sleeping with her?"

"No." The answer was sharper than necessary.

Tuck drew back and held up his palms in surrender.

"No," Shane repeated in a moderated tone. "And what makes you think I might be?"

"Because you practically challenged me to a duel over a dance. Did you see her again?"

"You mean after the search-and-rescue party?"

"Why are you answering my questions with questions?"

"Why are you?"

Tuck gave a reluctant chuckle. "You saw her again."

"Yes," Shane admitted.

"But nothing happened."

They hadn't slept together. But Shane found he didn't want Tuck to think it was platonic, either. "I wouldn't exactly say nothing."

"Ahhh…" Tuck's eyes lit with interest.

Shane immediately realized his mistake. He couldn't have it both ways, and he had no intention of elaborating. What he wanted was for Tuck to stay away from her.

"Justin interrupted us," he said. "And I found out I had to leave town. But I'm seeing her again next weekend."

"She seems pretty great," said Tuck.

Shane frowned at him. "You had your chance."

"I didn't exactly have a chance. But, you have dibs. I get that."

"I do have dibs," said Shane, focusing his attention on breakfast, cutting into the crispy waffle. "So, how exactly did you meet her?"

"I can't remember," Tuck answered. "Some social function or the other. I don't really know her all that well."

Shane was relieved to hear that.

"She's really down-to-earth," he said, smiling. "She's scared of dogs."

"Your dogs?"

"All dogs. Gus and Boomer about gave her a heart attack."

"You know your voice goes all soft when you talk about her. And your expression gets all moony eyed."

Shane glanced up. "Get lost."

"Don't shoot the messenger."

"She's refreshing," said Shane. "I'm so tired of the games women play, I can't even tell you."

"I hear you," said Tuck.

Tuck's phone rang on the table, and he glanced down. "Dixon and Kassandra are separating."

"What?" Shane drew back in surprise.

Tuck lifted the phone. "This is Dixon now."

Shane couldn't believe it. Tuck's older brother had been happily married for nearly ten years.

"Hey, Dix," Tuck said into the phone. He was silent at first, and then his expression sobered. "I'm in Paris. I flew over with Shane."

Shane took another bite of his waffle, while cataloguing the possible reasons behind what seemed like a sudden marriage breakup.

"You bet," said Tuck. "No, it's a great idea. We'll see you there." He ended the call and put down the phone.

"What happened?" asked Shane.

"He came home early from a business trip and caught her with some other guy," said Tuck. "It's as cliché as it comes."

"Kassandra had an affair?" Shane had a hard time wrapping his head around it. He knew Kassandra, had known her for years. She'd seemed incredibly devoted to Dixon.

"Dixon was ready to kill them both."

"No kidding." Shane couldn't imagine what he might do to a man who messed around with his wife. He couldn't even imagine what he'd do to a guy who messed around with Darci.

The thought brought him up short, and he shook off the ridiculous notion. They'd barely dated.

"Who's the guy?" he asked Tuck.

"Some midlevel executive from Resin Pharmaceutical."

"You don't think Dixon would really do him harm?" Shane couldn't bring himself to care about the stranger's fate, but he didn't want Dixon to get into any trouble.

"I sure hope not. He's coming to meet us here."

"In Paris?"

"He's in London." Tuck glanced at his watch. "Figures it'll take him an hour."

"I thought we had his jet?"

"We took *a* Tucker Transportation jet. But Dixon has his own."

"All to himself? All the time?"

"He's the face of the company, now that Dad's schedule is cut back. He needs to be where he needs to be."

As an only child, Shane sometimes wondered how Tuck felt about playing second fiddle to his older brother. He'd asked once, but Tuck had laughed the question off and moved the conversation to another topic.

"You own an aerospace company," said Tuck. "I can't believe you still fly commercial."

"We build planes. We don't operate them. And I'm a proud supporter of the commercial aviation industry."

"Your time is valuable."

"Everybody's time is valuable." Shane finished the last bite of his waffle. "What's Dixon going to do about Kassandra?"

"Divorce her, I assume."

Again, Shane tried to imagine how he'd feel in that situation. Darci seemed to be his benchmark all of a sudden.

Would he divorce her if she messed around? Okay, presupposing they'd gotten married first. Would he divorce her or just make the guy disappear and hope she fell back in love with him?

"Women," said Tuck with a disgusted shake of his head. He lifted his coffee cup.

Shane shut down the disturbing line of thought.

"Kassandra seemed like one of the good ones," he said to Tuck.

That someone like Bianca had betrayed Shane hadn't come as a huge surprise. Sure, the method and magnitude of her betrayal had been unexpected. But he'd dated her looking for fun, not for loyalty and commitment. But Kassandra had married Dixon, pledged to love and honor him.

"Just goes to show you," said Tuck.

"That you can't trust women?" asked Shane, his mind moving inexorably back to Darci. It would be nice to be able to trust at least one of them.

"That the sainted Dixon doesn't always make the right decisions," said Tuck.

Shane checked out his friend's tight expression. "Been holding that back for a while?"

Tuck drained his coffee cup. "You ready to go?"

"Tuck?" Shane prompted, wondering if Tuck wanted to open up about his brother.

"I told Dix we'd meet him at the airport," said Tuck.

Shane waited another moment but then let the subject drop. "We're picking him up?"

"Might as well. Unless you had something else in mind, maybe a romantic stroll along the Seine?"

"You're not as pretty as you think you are," Shane drawled.

Tuck grinned and tossed some euros on the table.

They left the hotel, and as their driver took them efficiently through the streets of Paris, Shane couldn't help but wonder some more about Tuck's relationship with his brother. Tuck was invariably respectful of Dixon, but there had to be resentment on some level. Why else would Tuck so studiously avoid becoming more involved in running the business?

Shane was tempted to ask outright, but the opportunity had passed, and Tuck was now giving an ad hoc tour of Paris, pointing out parks, cemeteries and countless historical buildings.

When they arrived at the private airport, Dixon's jet was taxiing from the runway.

The driver pulled the SUV to a halt, allowing Shane and Tuck to exit. After it came to a stop, the door of the Gulfstream yawned open, the staircase descended and Dixon emerged.

Their driver was quick to move forward in order to offer assistance, obviously sensing Dixon's importance.

"He's better at being a billionaire than we are," Shane said to Tuck as Dixon reached the bottom of the staircase, his haircut perfect, shoes polished to a shine, wearing a crisp, custom-made suit, with a leather overnight bag in his hand. Power and prestige seemed to exude from his pores.

"He does have a knack," said Tuck.

The driver took Dixon's bag and showed him to the SUV.

"Hey, bro," said Tuck, scrutinizing his brother's expression. "How are you holding up?"

"Thanks for coming," said Dixon, and he gave Tuck a brisk hug.

Shane felt a pang of envy. Whatever Tuck's feeling about their respective roles in Tucker Transportation, he clearly loved his brother.

Dixon gave Shane a nod. "Hey, Shane."

"Sorry to hear about Kassandra," said Shane, stepping up to shake Dixon's hand.

"Life can be unkind," said Dixon. "Then again, so was she. I hear the Gobrecht deal fell apart?"

"Unfortunately, yes," said Shane. "I'm here trying to save Beaumont."

The driver opened the front passenger door, and Dixon took the seat.

Shane and Tuck climbed into the back.

Dixon turned as the engine revved. "You taking another run at Gobrecht afterward?"

"There doesn't seem to be much point. Justin spent half the afternoon on the phone with them last week. I don't think it's salvageable."

"It's not, at least, not with a defeatist attitude like that," said Dixon.

"I prefer to think of it as realistic," said Shane.

The car exited the gates of the airport, and they turned onto the main road.

"You should go talk to them in person," said Dixon.

"I don't see how I'd even get an appointment," said Shane.

The last time they'd talked, the Gobrecht president had hung up on him.

Tuck sat silent in his seat, smirking at Shane being the object of Dixon's criticism.

"Show up on his doorstep," said Dixon.

"He has security."

Dixon shrugged. "It's worth a try, man. At the very least, it'll make an impression. And it'll give us something to do. God knows I'm in no hurry to get back to Chicago."

"I know some great nightclubs in Berlin," said Tuck. "Hottest women east of Stockholm."

"I'm—" Dixon stopped himself. "Yeah, I guess I'm not anymore."

"Do you know what you're going to do?" asked Shane, moving past the question of Gobrecht. Unlike Tuck, he wasn't compelled to take Dixon's advice.

"Blow the dust off the prenup and sic my lawyer on her."

"You're assets are protected?" asked Shane.

Tuck scoffed out a laugh. "The corporation's all Mom and Dad," he said.

"Shares don't come to us until Dad dies," Dixon added. "He always worried that some gold-digging woman would get her hands on Tucker Transportation. Never thought it would be Kassandra."

"So, your personal wealth…?" asked Shane, surprised to

learn he didn't already control a portion of Tucker Transportation.

Dixon shared a grin with Tuck. "Is trivial."

"Does Kassandra know that?"

"She will soon," replied Dixon.

"Women," said Tuck, "should come with a warning label."

Shane pictured Darci, her clear green eyes, her open smile, her auburn hair, tousled after he'd kissed her so long and so hard. What kind of a warning label would she wear?

Hot? Combustible? Handle With Care? Obsession Can Occur if Touched?

Yeah, that sounded about right.

Darci couldn't believe the plan had worked. The housekeeper had remembered her from the weekend and completely bought the story about her lost earring. She'd offered to help Darci look through the wine cellar, but Darci had insisted she could manage alone. When she'd said that Shane had shown her the key's hiding place, it had solidified her credibility.

She was beginning to think she might have a future in espionage, after all.

She first unlocked and left the door to the wine cellar ajar to keep the story credible, then she headed down the main hallway of the basement. Her heart was thudding in her chest, and her palms were breaking out in a sweat. But she forced herself to take all the side passages and open all the doors.

She was careful to make sure none of them led to the yard. The last thing she needed was a pair of monster dogs barreling toward her again. She was twenty minutes into her search, then thirty minutes, then thirty-five, when finally she hit pay dirt.

At the end of a secondary hallway, she found a big storage room. It had row upon row of industrial shelving. And on those shelves were file boxes, all labeled with the month and year.

She breathed a heartfelt sigh of relief, then quickly made her way along the cartons, following the chronology of the dates, going back to the very beginning of the company.

Then she found them. Boxes labeled D&I Holdings.

After a moment of elation, her heart sank. There had to be fifty containers. It would take her days to look through them all.

She heard voices in the distance, and her heart leapt to her throat. After a frozen second, she jumped to action, hit the light switch, slipped back into the corridor, closed the door behind her and rushed toward the main hallway.

Inside her head, she concocted a story about retracing her route with Shane. She'd tell them about the dogs getting in on the weekend and how she hadn't found the earring in the wine cellar, so now she was looking farther afield. She could keep a straight face while she told those lies. She had no choice.

The voices were male. They were coming closer. She held her breath.

But then the footsteps veered off, heading up the stairs to the main floor. The voices faded.

Darci nearly slumped to the floor in relief. She knew she should end this now, go back upstairs, tell the housekeeper she had found the earring and call it a day. But this was by far her best hope of finding something valuable. She couldn't imagine how she'd get another opportunity to be in the mansion without Shane.

She forced herself to go back into the storage room.

Her hand trembled as she reached for the light switch. She pulled it back to her body, rubbing it, telling herself to get a grip. Then she flicked on the lights.

As the fluorescents buzzed to life above her, she returned to the location of the D&I Holdings files. She pulled the oldest box from a shelf and opened the lid. Dust wafted through the air, and she waved it aside, peering at the neat rows of paper and file folders.

She found invoices and check stubs, rent, gas, water and power. The records showed the company had started in South Chicago in a leased warehouse that seemed to cost a fortune to heat. She came across invoices for used equipment, computers, tools, even workbenches and shelving. It was clear the two men had worked hard, cobbling together the equipment they needed to develop their early prototypes.

The records told a story, and she lost track of time until new voices startled her, and she jumped to her feet. There wasn't time to put everything back, so she went for the door, dashed out and shut it behind her.

"Miss Lake?" a woman's voice called in the distance.

Darci knew it had to be the housekeeper. She scrambled to the end of the hall and peeked around the corner.

"Miss Lake?"

"I'm here," Darci called out behind her. She struggled to keep from sounding breathless.

The housekeeper turned. "There you are. I got worried."

"I'm sorry," said Darci, walking forward. "I couldn't find it in the wine cellar. So I retraced my steps."

"Did you find it?"

"I did," said Darci, digging into the pocket of her jeans to produce the earring she'd planted there. "I'm so relieved. Did I tell you it was my grandmother's?"

"Yes," said the housekeeper, her critical gaze taking in Darci's clothing. "How did you get so dirty?"

Darci struggled not to panic. "I was down on the floor. It's so tiny." She held up the earring. "I can't believe I actually found it."

She couldn't help reflexively smoothing her hair. The lights were still on in the storage room, and she'd left records strewn all over the floor. She racked her brain for an excuse to stay downstairs.

Then she landed on one. "I'll just go lock up the wine cellar and meet you upstairs."

"I'll walk with you," said the housekeeper.

"No need," Darci quickly put in.

The quick retort earned her a suspicious gaze.

"It's no trouble," said the housekeeper, her expression implacable.

Darci guessed the housekeeper thought she was going to

steal a bottle of wine. And who could blame her? Darci knew she was acting as if she was up to something.

"Estelle?" came a man's voice.

"Down here, Mr. Massey," the housekeeper called in return.

"Oh, there you are." A tall, attractive thirty-something man strode toward them.

His gaze turned curiously to Darci. "Hello?"

"This is Darci Lake," said Estelle. "She visited Mr. Colborn on the weekend and lost an earring."

"Shane was nice enough to give me a tour of the wine cellar," Darci explained, ordering herself to remain calm.

"I'm Justin Massey," said the man. "Shane's attorney."

Darci's brain sputtered for a moment. She couldn't help thinking that if she got caught, this was the man who would grill her in court.

"Nice to meet you," she managed.

"Shane mentioned you."

"He did?" Darci searched Justin's expression for any trace of mistrust.

"All good, I assure you."

"Thank you." She relaxed ever so slightly.

"Did you find your earring?"

"I did." She held it out to prove it.

"Then that's good news."

"I was just going to lock up the wine cellar." She held her breath, hoping against hope that Justin would need Estelle's assistance.

"Estelle?" asked Justin, turning his attention away from Darci.

Yes, yes, yes! Darci's brain sang out.

"I need a couple of boxes from the file room."

No, no, no! This couldn't be happening. It couldn't. What were the odds?

"Is the trolley around?" he asked.

"Ben will know where it is," said Estelle. "I'll have him bring it over."

"Thanks, Estelle."

The woman produced a cell phone, moving slightly away to make the call.

"You work for Colborn Aerospace?" Darci asked Justin.

She was torn between attempting to stop him from entering the file room and running as fast and far as she could.

"Eight years now," said Justin.

"So you've known Shane all that time?"

"Longer," said Justin while Estelle's voice carried on in the background.

"I just met him," said Darci.

"At the fundraiser. I know. He seems to like you quite a lot."

"I like him, too." It was an honest answer. She did like Shane. She was out to discredit his father, not Shane himself.

"He told me you read the book."

"I was curious."

"It's mostly lies."

She fought an involuntary smile. "Are you his wingman?"

Justin shifted. "He doesn't usually need one."

"I don't imagine he does."

Shane was a charming, sexy billionaire. He could recite whatever he wanted in bed, and women would still line up around the block.

"Ben will be here shortly," said Estelle, coming back to them. "I'll help Miss Lake close up the wine cellar."

"No need," said Justin. "I can keep her company."

There was a brief appearance of discomfort on Estelle's face, but she promptly smoothed out her expression. Obviously, she wasn't about to disagree with Justin. But Darci had raised the woman's suspicions, and that had been a big misstep on her part.

"Thank you," Estelle said to Justin.

As she walked away, Justin turned to Darci. "I don't think she wanted to leave us alone."

Darci pretended she hadn't noticed. "Was that your take?"

"She probably thinks I'll make a pass at you."

Darci drew back in surprise. "What?"

Justin chuckled. "She's protecting Shane's interests."

"I don't think that's—"

"It's admirable," said Justin. "Loyalty is rare and valuable."

"I suppose," said Darci, realizing Justin's assumption was a whole lot safer than the truth.

"To the wine cellar?" he asked.

"I have the key."

As they made their way down the hall, Justin glanced at his watch. "We're well within the cocktail hour."

She assumed he was joking. "You're saying you'd steal Shane's wine?"

"In a heartbeat."

"You're his lawyer."

"As such, I'm declaring my power of attorney over his wine stash. I don't think it's too much of a stretch."

"It's too much of a stretch," said Darci. Though she couldn't help thinking an intoxicated Justin might give her a fighting chance at sneaking away to fix her mess in the records room.

"You have no sense of adventure," he said.

The comment startled a laugh out of her, which Darci quickly turned into a cough.

She couldn't try to get Justin drunk—on Shane's expensive wine—so she could snoop some more into his company records. Could she?

They arrived at the wine cellar, and she determinedly extracted the key. No. She wouldn't do that. She had to set some limits on her behavior.

"Last chance," he said.

"Close the door."

"I don't know if you're aware of some of the very rare vintages in here."

"Shane told me his father was a collector." She was careful to keep her tone neutral. But the wine was somehow emblematic of the differences in Dalton's and her father's circumstances.

"Dalton definitely liked the finer things in life."

"Did you know him?" Darci saw an opportunity for more information.

Justin nodded. "He was a brilliant, hardworking man."

"He built Colborn Aerospace all by himself?"

"Started with nothing but ideas."

Darci clamped her jaw, not trusting herself to speak.

"Went from a one-man shop to a ten-man shop, then a hundred, then a thousand. He was a tough man to work for, hard-nosed, exacting. Not everyone liked him."

"I'll bet," she said.

Justin pulled the heavy door shut, and she turned the key to lock it.

She crouched to secure the key behind the panel.

"Looks like he trusts you already," said Justin from above her.

She rose. "Do you mind showing me the records room?"

"Why?" he asked.

Because, if she was really, really lucky, he'd turn his back for a few minutes, and she'd have a chance to hide her mess.

To Justin, she gave a shrug. "This big old basement fascinates me. I'd like to see a little more of it."

"It'll be a disappointment after the wine cellar."

"I'll take my chances."

"Sure," he said. "Why not?"

Six

Shane had spent three days in Europe with Tuck and Dixon, visiting five potential customers, including Gobrecht. The Beaumont deal was shaky but still intact. The president of Gobrecht had agreed to meet with Shane, but then had said he was in talks with an up-and-coming firm named Ellis Air. Shane knew of Riley Ellis. They were both the same age, and both Chicago natives. But Ellis Air had never been a factor in the industry before now. He'd tried to explain the risks of going with such a small firm to Gobrecht, but they weren't in the mood to listen.

Now, back in Chicago and back at the mansion with Darci, he let the frustrations from the business trip slide away as she fed a biscuit to each of the dogs.

As Gus and Boomer gobbled them down, she took a half step back, glancing up at Shane, her expression a mixture of fear and pride.

"They're your friends for life," said Shane.

She glanced at the dogs. "They still look hungry."

"They always look hungry. Don't buy into it." He reached out and took her hand. "Let's walk."

The second the word *walk* was out, the dogs both bounded off in the usual direction.

"They like walks?" Darci asked on a laugh.

"They think it's their job to patrol the perimeter." He pointed to a bark-mulch path that wound through the gardens. "They love it when reinforcements come along."

The dogs raced out in front in the Sunday-morning sun. The air was warm. Robins were out in the oak trees, and the roses were coming into bloom. The lawn was freshly cut, the scent crisp around them.

Darci wore blue jeans, a mint-green tank top and a pair of ballet flats. Her thick auburn hair was pulled back in a ponytail, with strands flowing free at her temples. If she was wearing makeup, he couldn't tell. And her only jewelry was a pair of tiny gold earrings.

"Estelle said you lost an earring?" he asked while the dogs romped a few dozen yards ahead, crisscrossing the pathway, sniffing at the gardens along the way.

"An opal," said Darci, her gaze tracking Boomer. "My grandmother's. They have huge sentimental value for me. I don't have much that belonged to her. So I really appreciated the chance to come back and look for it. It took a while, and I had to check all over the place, but I eventually, you know, tracked it down… So I was happy."

"I'm glad to hear it," he said, smiling at her rush of words. "You met Justin?"

"I did." She drew in a very deep breath.

"He said you asked about the history of Colborn Aerospace."

"I did." She paused. "I was interested in the history."

"I know what you're doing."

Her hand twitched in his.

"And it's okay." He lifted the hand to kiss it. "I'd be curious about me, too. I'd probably be tempted to do a little research."

"I'm…" There was a thread of apprehension in her voice. "I mean, it's not…"

He'd clearly unnerved her. That hadn't been his intention. "I know you're not a gold digger, Darci."

She seemed to consider his words. "Right. Okay. How exactly do you know that?"

"Because gold diggers don't play hard to get."

Her expression faltered. "Is that what you think I'm doing?"

He backpedaled. "I don't mean to say you're doing it deviously. But you do call a halt whenever I get close."

"I do," she agreed.

"It's been my experience that when women are looking to set a trap for me, they don't say no to much of anything, climbing Mt. Logan, community trash pickup, mud wrestling."

"Mud wrestling?"

"I sometimes get creative to see how far women will go."

"You're nasty."

"They can always say no." He found himself smiling. "Like you do. And that's honest."

She wrinkled her nose while she shook her head. "I definitely won't be doing any mud wrestling."

He couldn't help but laugh.

"It's an offensive spectacle, full of bikinis and leering louts."

He tugged her to a halt and stepped in to face her. "Did I ask you to mud wrestle?"

"No."

"Have I ever pushed you to do something you truly didn't want to do?"

"Not with words."

"Nor coercion or money." He'd been nothing but respectful.

"True," she agreed.

"You just say no."

"I do."

"To anything that doesn't feel right."

Disquiet flitted through her eyes.

"What?" he asked.

"Nothing. I'm agreeing with you."

With the sun on her face, the breeze lifting her hair, the sheen of her lips, the subtle scent of her perfume, it all seemed straightforward to him.

"I want to kiss you," he said.

"Don't." She quickly put a palm against his chest.

"Don't kiss you, or don't *want* to kiss you?"

"Both." Her gaze held his, and the air seemed to heat between them.

"Why?" he asked. They'd kissed a couple of times. "It's just a kiss. How can it not feel right?"

She seemed to have to think it through, and he took that as a good sign.

"It's not always that things don't feel right in the moment," she said. "Sometimes things feel right, and I say no anyway.

Because they're not right. And they can never be right. And it doesn't matter how much I want them to be."

"Darci." He put his hand over hers, struggling to keep his expression serious. "Did that make sense inside your head?"

She tugged her hand away. "You're mocking me?"

"Because you're overthinking."

"I'm not."

"I still want to kiss you."

"Well, I don't want to kiss you."

"You're lying."

She hesitated. "It doesn't matter. Can we just walk?"

"Yes." He stepped to her side and took her hand again.

They strolled in silence while he dissected her words. Something was off. Something was wrong, but he couldn't figure out what it was.

He took a stab. "You're not married, are you?"

"Let it go, Shane."

"Seriously? You're married?"

"I'm not married."

"Ever been married?"

"No. You?"

"You don't think you'd have found that online?"

Gus did a circle around them, dodging between them, then loping off.

"I suppose," she said.

"I checked you out, too," he told her. "Didn't find much."

"I try to keep a low profile."

"Are you in the witness protection program?"

"Something like that."

Was that it? Had he nailed it?

"Are you in danger?" he asked. "Because if that's it, if you are, I have resources—"

"I'm not in any danger."

"An old boyfriend?" he asked. "Is he jealous? A stalker? Is that why you were asking about security?"

"I wasn't asking about security. You told me about your security."

"Then you asked for details."

She gave a wordless exclamation of frustration. "There's no stalker ex-boyfriend. Jeez, Shane. Kissing you is starting to look a lot better than talking to you."

It was all the invitation he needed, and he didn't hesitate for a second. He spun her around, latched an arm across the small of her back, tugged her in and pressed his lips to hers.

She went still with shock. But then her body softened. Her lips parted, and she kissed him back.

Okay. So that was the answer. The direct approach.

He enfolded her deeper into his embrace, widened the kiss and teased her tongue out with his. Her curves were delectable, her breasts pressed against his chest, her skin hot against his.

One of the dogs zipped past, brushing the back of his legs, but he ignored it, bracing his feet apart to hold her steady.

Then both dogs barked, and she broke the kiss. "Oh, no."

"It's just a kiss."

"We can't do this."

"We didn't do anything." He'd wanted to do something. He wanted to do a whole lot. He'd wanted to haul her off into the pool house and make frantic love to her for the rest of the day.

"We're playing with fire."

Again, he struggled to figure her out. Who cared if they were playing with fire? What was the worst that could happen?

She was clearly attracted to him. And she was obviously a healthy, sexy, amazing woman. What could be holding her back?

He racked his brain for a plausible explanation.

"Are you saving yourself for marriage?" he asked.

"No. No, that's not it."

"Then what is it?" He found himself growing impatient, an edge coming into his voice.

She withdrew her arms and stepped back.

He could have kicked himself.

"I wish I could explain," she said.

"You *can* explain."

"No, I can't. I really have to go."

"If your plan is to intrigue me, I'm intrigued already."

She backed away, shaking her head. "I thought I could do this."

"Do *what*?" Baffled was too mild a word for what he was feeling.

"I'm sorry." She turned.

"What did I say?" he called. "What did I do?"

But she was leaving. Her brisk stride turned into a jog.

He took a first step, intent on going after her. But he knew it was useless. There was nothing more he could say, and he'd be wrong to press her.

He had to step back, to think this through, to figure out what was holding her back and how to fix it.

Darci rushed through the apartment door to find Jennifer standing in the kitchen.

"I can't do this," she blurted, tossing her purse on the nearest chair. "I'm going to crack. I can tell. I can feel it."

"Crack?" asked Jennifer, an ice-cream scoop in her hand and a carton of chocolate-ribbon cookie-dough on the counter.

Darci paced to the breakfast bar. "I went to Shane's again."

"I know. But you said you were going to stay in the yard. What happened? Did you find anything?"

"I found out that I'm weak willed."

Jennifer scoffed out a laugh and dug into the ice cream, placing a second scoop in a glass dessert bowl. "Is that all? Join the club."

"Are you particularly hungry?" Darci asked, realizing Jennifer was going to town on their favorite gourmet flavor.

"Starving. You want some?"

On balance, it seemed like a good idea. "Definitely." Darci moved to the breakfast bar and hopped up on a stool.

Jennifer pulled another bowl from beneath the counter and filled it with two generous scoops. "Whipped cream?"

"Yes." Darci took in Jennifer's jerky movements and tight expression. "Wait a minute, is everything okay?"

"You first. What's about to make you crack?"

"Shane."

In response, Jennifer sprayed a generous flourish of whipped cream into each bowl. She stuck a spoon into the middle of one and pushed it across the counter to Darci.

"What happened with you?" asked Darci, rescuing the spoon before it could fall sideways.

"Ashton." Jennifer took a huge bite of her own sundae.

Alarm bells went off in Darci's brain. "Uh-oh."

"He called." Jennifer took another big bite.

"What did he say?"

"He asked me out. Tonight. He has a reservation at Mystique and tickets to Rainbow Quarter, fifth row, center. Do you know how hard those are to get?"

"You can't sell your soul for fifth-row, center seats to Rainbow Quarter."

Jennifer began eating the ice cream with gusto, her voice full of self-disgust. "That's not the problem."

Darci waited.

Jennifer looked up. "Problem is I'd sell my soul for a burger and nosebleed seats at minor-league softball."

"You *can't*—" Darci stopped herself, remembering how she'd felt when Shane kissed her today. "Never mind," she said. "You shouldn't. But I totally get it."

She shoved a spoonful of the concoction into her mouth. The whipped cream had started to liquefy, but it was still delicious and a satisfying balm to her frayed nerves.

"Explain," said Jennifer.

"I nearly jumped into bed with Shane Colborn this morning."

Jennifer's brows shot up.

Darci took another mouthful of the sweet indulgence. "He kissed me," she said. "Again. And it was like… It was…"

"Like being swept up on an avalanche of chocolate-dipped hormones?"

"That's pretty close."

"Sucks, doesn't it?" asked Jennifer.

"Big-time. Tell me you said no."

"I said no."

"To Ashton," Darci confirmed.

"Yes. What else would I be talking about?"

"Nothing. Good. Stick to your guns."

Time ticked by while they ate.

"What are you going to do?" Jennifer asked.

"For you, is it like some kind of overpowering, magnetic force?" Darci asked.

Spoon in her mouth, Jennifer nodded. "That's why it's scary."

"Well, I can't go back to the mansion," said Darci.

They both ate in silence for a few more minutes.

"Unless you used it," said Jennifer.

Darci didn't understand. "Used what?"

"Used your attraction to Shane as a tool to spy on him."

Darci still didn't understand. "How would I do that?"

"Give in and go for it. The guy will eventually fall asleep. They all do."

Darci couldn't believe she was hearing right. She also couldn't help imagining sleeping with Shane.

A calculating smile grew on Jennifer's face. "You could wear him out completely, make him sleep for hours. I could give you some tips."

Darci shook her spoon admonishingly, as much at herself as at Jennifer. "I don't need tips. And I'm *not* going to wear Shane out with sex."

"Kill two birds," said Jennifer.

Darci ordered herself to ignore the outrageous idea. "Maybe the drawings are at the office. I'm going to focus there for a while."

"Sometimes I wish you were less moral."

"Are you saying you'd sleep with Shane in this circumstance?" Darci didn't believe it for a second.

"I'd sure sleep with Ashton for the cause."

"That's completely different. You *wish* you could sleep with Ashton for any cause."

"True enough." Jennifer seemed to consider their situations. "You could always throw in the towel."

"You mean give up fighting my attraction to Shane." The more she said it out loud, the more it seemed conceivable, and that was frightening.

Jennifer grinned knowingly. "No. I meant give up hunting for your father's drawings. That's another option."

"Oh." Darci scooped up a bite.

Then Jennifer's expression sobered, turning thoughtful. "Maybe it's time to let the professionals take over. You could hire a private detective. Or check with a lawyer. If the Colborns ripped your dad off, there has to be a way to get a subpoena for the schematic drawings."

"I'm afraid to tip them off."

It took Jennifer a second to understand. "Because they might find and destroy the drawings?"

"This all happened decades ago, before we scanned and emailed copies of everything. One lighted match to the originals, and poof."

"But you might never find them on your own. And you could go to jail for looking."

"I haven't broken any laws." Darci frowned. "At least not any significant ones. They don't throw you in jail for party crashing or snooping."

"They might throw you in jail for theft."

"If it gets to that point and Shane charges me with theft of corporate records, I'll charge him with theft of intellectual property. We'll see who blinks first."

"That only works if you can find the drawings."

"I'll find them," Darci said, digging deep for her earlier confidence. "They have to be somewhere. I'll start fresh by scouring every corner of Colborn headquarters."

Jennifer polished off the last of her ice cream. "Is there anything I can do to help?"

There wasn't.

"Is there anything I can do to help with Ashton?" Darci asked in return.

As she finished the sentence, Jennifer's phone rang.

"Let me talk to him this time," said Darci.

"It's not going to be—" Jennifer glanced at the screen. "It's him."

"Hand it over."

Jennifer drew a steadying breath and held out the phone

Darci accepted it, pressing the answer button and holding it to her ear. "She can't talk to you, Ashton."

"Darci?"

"Yes, it's Darci. You have to back off."

"This is none of your business." Ashton's deep tone was unyielding.

"She's my best friend."

"Darci—"

"I can't let you hurt her."

"All I want to do is explain."

"You've already explained. You're a recovering narcissist. She gave you a second chance, and you hurt her again. "

"It's not what you think."

"It's exactly what we think."

"I didn't—" Ashton sucked in a loud breath. "Put her on the phone."

"No."

"It's not your decision to make."

"You're right. It's Jennifer's decision, and she made it. Goodbye, Ashton. Have a nice life." Darci hit the end button.

"Wow," said Jennifer with a note of awe.

"You must have said all those things before."

"Not so succinctly."

"I was trying to be definitive."

"You were definitely definitive."

"Good. Maybe he'll back off."

Jennifer worried her bottom lip for a moment. "Maybe."

Darci could all but read her mind.

Jennifer's emotions were at war with her logic. Darci got it now. She hadn't before, but her jumbled-up feelings for Shane helped her understand. Ashton might be the worst man in the world for Jennifer, but she was in deep and she couldn't quite bring herself to walk away.

She scraped the bottom of her dessert bowl. "I think we're going to need more ice cream."

Shane couldn't pinpoint exactly when he'd lost control of his own life, but it was definitely gone.

"There are at least three news reporters waiting out front," said Justin as they headed along the hallway of the executive floor of the Colborn building, midafternoon on Monday.

Shane ignored Justin's words, focused on more important things than reporters. "That's when I realized even the chauffer couldn't help me," he said, beyond frustrated with the Darci situation.

"The *Morning Rise* television show," Justin continued on his own train of thought. "*The Circle* magazine and something called *Sax On-Line*, which focuses on celebrity gossip."

"He actually dropped her off at a cafe on Elm," said Shane. "He didn't take her to her apartment. Who does that? And how did I not get her phone number?"

Shane had belatedly realized he and Darci had set up all their plans in person. He should have thought to put her number into his cell, but he hadn't. It wasn't something he normally missed. After she left yesterday, he'd searched online for her contact information and had drawn a blank.

"Riley Ellis announced the deal with Gobrecht in front of a dozen microphones," said Justin. "Now Bianca's saying it's further proof she was telling the truth in her book."

"She's got no online presence," said Shane. "None. Nothing." How did a person live like that?

"Bianca?" asked Justin.

"Darci."

"Have you heard a word I've said?" asked Justin.

"Have you heard a word *I've* said? I don't know how I'm going to contact her." There was an outside chance Shane wouldn't be able to contact her. There was a slim but frightening chance she was gone from his life.

"If you talk to a reporter, we could lose Beaumont."

Shane dragged himself back to business. "And if I don't talk to a reporter?"

"We could lose Beaumont."

"Then it doesn't really matter what I do, does it?"

Justin stopped in his tracks. "What is wrong with you?"

Shane halted, turning to stare down his lawyer.

Justin nodded at the few people passing by. He stepped closer, moderating his tone. "This is serious."

"Fine. It's serious. What do you want me to do?"

"Go back to France. Hand hold while they sign on the dotted line."

The last thing Shane wanted to do was leave the country again. He needed to keep looking for Darci.

"This isn't a good time."

"Yeah? When would be a good time for you? After the bankruptcy proceedings?"

"Don't be so alarmist."

"Don't be such an idiot."

Justin was right. Justin was smart. And Shane's head was getting all messed up.

Fine, if he had to go to France, he'd go to France. But he'd do it as fast as humanly possible. "I want a corporate jet."

Justin gave his head a shake as if to clear it.

"If I'm going to be bopping across the Atlantic with this much regularity, I want to fly private."

In response, Justin pressed a button on his phone and raised it to his ear. "Ginger? Shane's going to need a corporate jet. Tomorrow. Two, maybe three days in Europe." He paused. "Thanks."

"It was Tuck's idea," said Shane, not sure why he felt he had to justify the request. "But Dixon made some good points, too. Private is faster, more efficient, more flexibility."

"You want a jet, we'll get you a jet. We'll use a service for now. But you can have one permanently if it makes you happy."

"How did I not get her phone number?"

Justin pressed the elevator button. "You can't go out the front door."

"I know."

Justin checked the knot on his tie and straightened his suit jacket. "She can't be that hard to track down."

"That's what I thought. But there's no Darci Lake listed in all of Chicago."

They stepped onto the elevator.

"Social media?" asked Justin.

"Not that I can find."

"Facial recognition? Got any photos?"

"Tuck," said Shane as inspiration hit. "Tuck knows her."

The elevator descended toward the basement level.

Justin went back to his phone. "The reporters are probably tailing your driver. But I'll get a cab to meet us at the back entrance."

"This is ridiculous. I'm not some hot rock star."

"I know."

"And I have nothing to hide."

"You're in a bad mood. It's too easy for them to get a sound bite."

"I'm not in a bad mood."

"Ha."

The elevator door opened at the basement level.

"It's not because of Bianca," said Shane. "And it's not Gobrecht."

"I know."

"It's—" Shane blinked and stopped dead.

He couldn't believe it.

It was impossible.

But, there she was, standing outside the records center in his basement.

The elevator door started to close on them. His hand snapped out to stop it.

"Shane?" asked Justin.

"Darci?" Shane called out.

She turned.

When she saw him, her jaw dropped. The color drained from her face, and she gripped the lip of the counter.

He strode quickly forward, grasping her hands, making sure she was real.

"What's going on?" he asked. "Why are you here?" He forced himself to change course. "I mean, it's *great* to see you."

"Darci," came a sharp, disapproving female voice.

Darci glanced up, her expression a study in guilt and panic.

Shane turned to see Rachel Roslin, his records manager bearing down on them.

The second she recognized Shane, her entire demeanor changed. "Mr. Colborn, sir. Can I help you with something?"

Shane looked back at Darci. That was when he spotted a file folder tucked under her arm. And that she was wearing a straight, navy skirt and a matching blazer. She looked…

She was working. She worked here. She *worked* at Colborn Aerospace.

Everything came together inside his head.

He instantly released her hands.

Justin had obviously reached the same conclusion and stepped in to distract Rachel. "We're avoiding the media," he told her. "A cab is picking us up out back."

"Of course," Rachel answered, still glancing suspiciously in Darci's direction. "I understand."

"I'll need to borrow Darci," said Shane.

The woman seemed stunned by the unusual request.

"We need some, uh, records support for an offsite meeting."

It took Rachel a second to find her voice. "Certainly, sir. But I'd be happy to personally provide you with any—"

Again, Justin stepped up. "We wouldn't want to take you away from your busy job. Truth is we need someone only for cosmetic reasons. The other party will bring along an entourage, and we want to even things out. Make Shane look important, you understand."

"I certainly do," said Rachel. "Darci, please go with Mr. Colborn and Mr. Massey." She gave a decisive nod to end the command.

Darci hadn't uttered a word.

"Do you need to get your purse?" Shane asked her.

She met his gaze, blinking with what looked like abject terror.

He wanted to tell her not to worry. Nothing was going to happen to her job.

She gave a shaky nod. Then she ducked her head and scooted off.

Shane felt an irrational urge to go after her. He couldn't shake the fear he might lose her again. But he was standing next to both the basement exit and the elevators. She had no choice but to come back to him.

Rachel Roslin left as well.

"What is this?" Justin whispered under his breath.

"It explains why she didn't want to sleep with me."

"Really? Your ego is the first place you go with this?"

"It's not ego. It wasn't making sense." All the signs had said she was attracted to Shane.

Justin snorted out a laugh. "Not all women want to sleep with you."

"This one does."

Justin shot him an incredulous look.

"Believe me or not, I don't care. Here she comes."

Shane's vision tunneled to Darci as she made her way down the short hallway. He'd found her again. Nothing else mattered.

Seven

They were three blocks away from the office, and Darci was growing more jumpy by the second. Suddenly, their cab pulled to the curb behind a black SUV.

"We're evading the press by taking a cab and going the back way," said Shane, taking her hand in his and whisking her from one vehicle to the other. "I think it's overkill, but they were camped out at the front entrance."

He hadn't asked any questions yet, and she'd done nothing but try to keep all-out panic at bay.

Her mind was whirling a million miles a minute. She was caught. It was over. And Shane had to be furious.

"I was on my way to a meeting," he said. "But Justin will cancel."

She realized Justin had stayed in the taxi, and the SUV was in motion. Shane deployed the privacy screen to separate them from the driver.

Darci's throat went dry, and sweat prickled her skin as Jennifer's dire warnings flashed through her mind. She couldn't believe Shane would harm her. Then again, if he thought his family fortune was at stake, could she be sure?

She battled an urge to escape, to jump from the vehicle, onto the sidewalk and flee. She could do that at the next red light. She spied the door handle, only a foot from her right hand.

"Time to come clean," he said.

She swallowed.

"Is *that* what this is all about?" His voice seemed to boom in the small space.

She turned her head, shrinking back toward the door.

His waited, and his brow creased in annoyance. "Was it?"

She opened her mouth, but all she could manage was an inarticulate rasp.

"I get it," he said, in a now softer voice. "Okay, I get it."

Heart pounding loudly in her chest, she tried to make sense of his words.

"But I hate that you lied," he continued. "You should have been straight with me."

"I…" She struggled to speak, trying to decide where to start.

"That first night, sure. But afterward?"

"I was afraid," she managed.

"I get that you don't want to sleep with the boss. I would have understood that. But I can't help you, we can't work this out if I don't even know the problem."

Did he know the problem? If he knew the real problem, he surely wouldn't be suggesting they could work things out.

"You had me second-guessing everything." He gave a self-deprecating laugh.

"I didn't mean to do that." She waited on pins and needles, afraid to even *hope* this was only about her job.

"I don't know why Tuck didn't tell me you worked for Colborn."

"Tuck didn't know," she said, still waiting for Shane to call her out for spying.

"How could he not know?"

"I didn't tell him. I don't really know him all that well."

"He said you had your own business, a website-design company."

"I do. But that's only part-time." Her heart rate began to moderate, and she tried to even out her breathing.

Shane thought the fact that she worked for him explained her erratic behavior. And it did. Or it could.

He shifted in his seat, angling more fully toward her. "Let's start over."

She didn't understand. "With this conversation?"

"With this *relationship*."

They didn't have a relationship. She didn't *want* a relationship. But she gave a hesitant nod anyway, knowing it was her way out for the moment. Relief warred with guilt inside her chest.

"What worries you most?" he asked, the concern in his

expression ratcheting up the guilt side of the equation. "Publicity, job security, gossip?"

She tried to frame an answer. If she was a regular employee getting involved with the president, all of those things would worry her. But in her true circumstance, none of them mattered.

Then a sudden grin burst out on Shane's face. "I've got it. It's perfect."

"What?"

"Tuck can give you a job."

"What?"

"That'll fix everything." Shane spoke with mounting enthusiasm. "You won't work for me anymore, so our personal relationship can't ever impact your employment. It'll take care of the gossip, though we can still be as discreet as you like."

"Whoa." She had to shut this down right away. "I don't want to work for Tuck."

"Why not?" Shane looked confused. "You keep saying you never had a relationship with him."

"I *didn't* have a relationship with him."

"Then why don't you want to work for him? I can easily get you a substantial raise. I'll make sure you don't lose out on any benefits or vacation time."

She knew it was a reasonable solution. And she didn't have a credible answer. As a lowly file clerk, what did it matter which large conglomerate employed her?

Luckily, the car pulled to a halt at the curb, giving her a reprieve.

"Where are we?" she asked, to change the subject, making a show of peering out the window.

"The penthouse." He reached for the door handle. "We can talk up there."

"Your penthouse?"

"Who else's? We can't go out together in public. I understand that. I have to say I wondered why you seemed to like the mansion so much. Good call on your part."

Fear of publicity wasn't why she liked the mansion. But

Shane seemed incredibly adroit at making this new cover story work for her.

He took her hands in his, capturing her gaze. His eyes were deep, dark and sincere, his baritone voice soothing. "I'm not going to press you, Darci. This isn't about sleeping together. But we either work this out, or we have to walk away from each other. And I can't simply walk away from you."

Once again, guilt threatened to engulf her. "You shouldn't be like this."

"Like what?"

"I don't know… So…compassionate."

He smiled. "I'm not compassionate. You've read the book."

"You don't sync with the book." He didn't sync with any of her expectations.

"Can I quote you on that?"

"Sure, you can. 'Colborn Aerospace file clerk defends reputation of its president.' I think that'll change a lot of minds."

His smile widened. "Let's go up and talk."

She didn't seem to have a choice but to go to his penthouse. She scrambled to make it okay in her mind. She told herself she could gather more information. There could be clues in his penthouse, corporate secrets, company history.

A doorman let them into the opulent building, then Shane swiped a key card inside the elevator. They were swept up thirty-two floors, where the doors opened onto a private, marble-floored foyer.

As they walked inside, Darci gazed around an expansive living room with two entire walls of glass overlooking the lake. The sofas were cream-colored leather, which contrasted with a pair of matching black armchairs. The tables were glass topped, and the space was accented with simple, but expensive-looking lamps and earthy, ceramic art.

"Nice view," she said as her feet sank into the plush carpet. She felt pulled toward the huge windows.

"It's great on a clear night," he answered. "Not so great in the fog."

"I'm sure you suffer greatly in inclement weather."

He came up behind her. "Are you mocking me?"

"I am."

"Fair enough. I have nothing to complain about. The view is great any time of day." His tone softened. "I'd love for you to see the sunrise."

She knew she should counter, come back with a stinging retort. But she couldn't think of anything.

"I'm sorry. I shouldn't have said that."

For an indulgent moment, she didn't care. She wanted to turn into his arms, kiss him deeply, get swept away with passion until the sun came up in the morning.

His hands now rested on her shoulders. The touch was light, but she felt the urgent desire right to her toes. She couldn't bring herself to shrug away.

He stroked her hair. His lips met her neck, kissing once, then twice.

"I'm lying," he muttered. "I'm not at all sorry. You are so beautiful."

She closed her eyes and relaxed against him, feeling his heat and the strength that supported her body. Resistance left her.

His kisses grew bolder, hotter, leaving damp circles in their wake.

She moved her head to one side, giving him better access, letting colors glide behind her eyes. He tugged her blazer down her arms, tossing it aside.

He moved to be in front of her and then cradled her face in his palms.

She opened her eyes to meet his gaze.

"I've missed you," he whispered.

"We're going to regret this." She had to say it out loud.

"Maybe someday." His voice was a low growl. "But it's going to take a while."

His lips captured hers, and she melted into the sensations. He was pure male heat and she didn't want to stop. She didn't want to question. She kissed him back, her tongue tangling with his in a way that already felt familiar.

His hand delved into her hair. The other went to her waist, drawing her closer, pressing them intimately together.

Between them, his phone vibrated and rang.

She jumped.

"Forget it," he rasped and resumed kissing her.

"Do you—?"

"No." He shrugged out of his jacket, dropping it, phone and all onto a chair. "There's nothing in the world more important than you."

Her last scrap of resistance fled. She ran her palms along his chest.

He smoothed back her hair and again cradled her face, his voice a breathless whisper. "Darci."

"Shane."

"Is this okay? Do you want to say no?"

"I'm not saying no. I'm through saying no." This was what she wanted, she knew it absolutely.

"Thank goodness."

She expected him to kiss her, but he gazed into her eyes instead.

"What?" she finally asked.

"Just savoring the moment."

She found herself smiling in return. "You risk me having second thoughts."

"No, I don't." He popped the top button on her blouse. "You're not going to have second thoughts."

"What an ego."

He popped the next one. He ran his other hand around the back of her neck. "You've made up your mind. This is real."

She shivered with reaction.

"When I touch you, you light up. Your eyes glow like emeralds. Your cheeks flush pink. And you get these amazing little goose bumps all over your skin. I've had women fake it before…" He kissed her.

She opened to his taste, reveling in the tiny shockwaves moving through her body, setting off pulses of desire deep in her core.

Before she knew it, her blouse was off. It was followed by his shirt and then her bra. They were skin to skin, their hands enthusiastically exploring each other.

He was rock-solid muscle, from his biceps and shoulders to his chest and abs. The musk of his skin teased her senses while his touch ignited every spot his fingers encountered.

His hand closed over her bare breast, and she moaned with deep satisfaction. His mouth followed the path of his hand, and she struggled to stay balanced. He kissed her belly, unbuttoning her slacks and slipping them down.

She stepped out of her shoes, and he peeled off her panties.

He kissed the inside of her thigh, and she grasped his shoulders for support, her grip on reality truly slipping away.

By the time he rose, she was entranced.

He quickly got rid of the rest of his clothes, found a condom and then he lowered himself to a sofa, drawing her down to straddle his lap. Their bodies met intimately.

"I want you," he rasped. "So, so bad."

Their gazes locked, and slowly he flexed his hips, going deeper and deeper. Her body claimed his, her heart thudding hard as she gasped for breath.

He paused and his hands slid up her thighs, sending a pulse ricocheting through her.

He leaned up and captured her lips. She wanted more, so much more, and wrapped her arms around him to hold him close.

"I'll want you always and forever," he whispered against her mouth.

"Sure," she agreed, and suddenly shifted her body against his, moving over him.

He groaned in reaction. With his hands bracing her, he pulled her to him, his own body arching.

The world blurred out, as she lost track of time. Nothing mattered, nothing existed outside of their lovemaking.

He kissed her lips, her cheek, her chin, her neck.

She held on tight, inhaling the dusky scent of his hair.

His rhythm increased. Her body sang and stiffened.

He deftly shifted her onto her back. Sensation spun onto a whole new level. Too soon, she was calling his name and diving over the edge to oblivion.

"Darci," he gasped. "Darci, Darci."

He slowed and went still, his weight satisfying on top of her. Aftershocks twitched over her skin while her lungs struggled for air.

She could feel his heartbeat, his lungs expanding in his chest.

His breath puffed against her ear.

Reality was out there somewhere, but she was in no hurry to find it.

Darci's body was sweet and slick beneath his own, her soft curves cradling him. His breathing returned to normal, and his heart rate stabilized. But he had no desire to move.

He felt an urge to apologize. This wasn't what he'd planned. He knew he hadn't pressured her, but they hadn't talked much at all, more like leaped into each other's arms.

He eased back to look at her. Her lips were bright red, slightly swollen, and her eyes were still luminous beneath her dark lashes. He brushed the pad of his thumb across her flushed cheek.

"Hey," he said softly.

"Hey," she returned, a hesitant smile on her face.

"I didn't mean it to happen that way."

"What way did you mean it to happen?"

"Candlelight, wine, a bed, maybe some flowers."

"Maybe stay dressed for more than three minutes after the penthouse door closed behind us?"

"Maybe," he admitted, then gave in to a smile. "Maybe not."

Tenderly, he touched his forehead to hers. "Ah, Darci. What do you do to me?"

"I wasn't trying to do anything." There was a note of unease in her voice.

He drew back. "I know that. You simply breathe and I want you."

"I could stop."

"Not advisable."

He knew he had to get up. He had to be heavy on top of her. What he really wanted to do was kiss her all over again and let passion take them where it would. But he'd be a gentleman.

A little late, but he'd give it a shot.

"I have a very roomy shower," he said, "or a couple of robes, or a hot tub on the deck and some very fine wine."

It was a moment before she spoke. "I do like a fine wine."

He smiled as his phone rang again.

"I should have thrown that thing against the wall."

"It might be important," she said.

"I don't care."

It rang again.

She craned her neck to look behind them. "Can you reach it?"

He wasn't about to try. "Am I too heavy? Should I move?"

"You're going to miss the call."

"That's true. Am I hurting you?"

"I can't tell. I've gone numb."

He quickly removed his weight.

But she smiled, clearly teasing.

He scooped her onto his lap. "My vote is for the hot tub and wine."

There was reluctance in her expression, but after a minute, she nodded.

He took her hand, and they rose. They moved to the section of his patio screened by a stone wall, plants and lattice work. There, he helped her into the water and turned the switch for the jets.

"Wait here," he said. "I'll be right back."

She sank down into the frothy blue water. "I doubt I'll be going anywhere."

She looked relaxed, and he relaxed, too.

While he was opening the wine, his phone rang again. This time, he checked the display. It was Justin.

He put it on speaker and continued twisting the corkscrew. "What's up?"

"Hi. How'd it go?"

"Fine. We're talking." He popped the cork out of the bottle.

"Still?" Justin sounded surprised.

Shane checked his watch—nearly six. "There's a lot to say."

"Like what?"

"Yeah, right. What do you need?" Shane took two long-stemmed glasses from the hanging rack above the countertop.

"Jet's all set up for tomorrow."

Shane had forgotten about the trip to France. "Damn."

"Why damn? What's going on there?"

"Nothing. I just don't feel like spending the next nine hours on a plane."

"The jet has a bedroom. You can overnight and sleep en route."

Shane's gaze strayed to Darci. He could just make out the back of her head in the tub. He wondered if she'd like to come to France.

"Anything else you need from me?" he asked Justin.

"Other than saving the Beaumont deal and possibly the future of Colborn Aerospace?"

"I meant in the next few hours."

"You've got something planned for the next few hours?" Justin teased.

"Quit fishing for details."

"Toss me a bone. I'm stuck talking to accountants."

"Have fun." Shane hit the end button. He abandoned the phone. Taking the wine bottle in one hand and the glasses in the other, he joined Darci outside.

"Chateau Montagne 1999," he said as he poured at a small cedar table.

"Should I be impressed?"

"You should." He handed her a glass.

"Expensive?" she asked. –

"It is, but that's not the most important factor."

"What is the most important factor?"

"It's delicious."

She grinned. "Then I'm impressed."

He set his glass on the edge of the tub and climbed in, facing her. "And my mission is complete."

Her expression faltered.

"My mission to impress you with wine," he quickly added. "Not—"

"To have sex with me?"

"*No.* That wasn't a mission."

She waited.

"It was a…an aspiration."

"Semantics."

He wasn't going to lie. He'd wanted her in his bed from the first night he'd met her. His feelings hadn't changed, but it was more complicated now.

"It's the cosmetics of the situation, right?" he asked, wanting to be certain of her concerns.

"The cosmetics?"

"You're worried that it will look like you're sleeping your way to the top, or that I coerced you into my bed."

Her tone turned flippant. "Am I sleeping my way to the top?"

"Darci."

"Where exactly is the top?"

"Stop it. I'm not worried about your behavior. I'm worried about mine." He couldn't live with himself if he'd inadvertently said or done anything that made her feel compelled to sleep with him.

"You're already at the top, Shane."

She was evading the question, and it triggered a reflexive alarm bell. *Had* she felt compelled to sleep with him?

He wanted to be crystal clear. "If I wasn't your boss, if I wasn't president of Colborn, would you be here?"

"If you weren't president of Colborn Aerospace, I never would have crashed your party and met you."

"You crashed my party?"

Her expression faltered again. "File clerks weren't on the invitation list."

He slowed down the conversation with a sip of his wine. He had to think about this. He didn't want to default to suspicion, but their initial meeting hadn't been accidental.

"You didn't answer the question," he couldn't help but note.

His worry had now switched from him accidentally coercing her to her deliberately manipulating him. He truly hated having this conversation, but he wasn't about to get duped again.

"Would you be here if I wasn't a billionaire?" he asked.

She was silent for so long that he feared he was right.

"Shane, the biggest downside to me sleeping with you is that you're the billionaire president of Colborn Aerospace."

"You're not looking to marry rich?"

"Do you want me to leave?"

"I want you to answer the question."

"No. I'm not looking to marry rich. And if I was, I'd probably lie about it, so this interrogation is next to useless."

"I know you'd lie," said Shane. People lied to him all the time. "It's not what you say that counts. I'm gauging your expression and intonation."

Her jaw snapped tight. "You know, if I wasn't naked, I'd probably storm out of here in some grand, self-righteous exit."

"Then thank goodness you're naked."

For a second, he thought he'd gone too far.

But to his surprise, instead of leaving she took up her wine.

"You're right not to trust people," she said. "They're inherently untrustworthy. Everyone's got an agenda."

Now she had him intrigued. "Do you have an agenda?"

"Absolutely."

"Will you share it with me?"

She gazed at her glass. "In the short term, my agenda has a lot to do with Chateau Montagne."

"So, you're not angry?"

"That you're a suspicious man?" She shook her head. "No."

She was both surprising and refreshing. Just when he thought he had her pegged, she'd take a sharp left and throw him off balance. This was definitely a woman worth getting to know.

"How do you feel about France?" he asked.

"As a wine-making country?"

"As a tourism destination. Paris, specifically."

"What's not to like about Paris?"

"Have you ever been there?"

The question seemed to amuse her. "I have not."

He took the plunge. "I'm going to Paris on business tomorrow. Want to come along?"

"I have to work."

"I can take care of that."

"See, that's exactly what we're *not* going to do. I'm not ditching work and flying across the Atlantic with the big boss."

"You need to take that job with Tuck."

"Shane, you barely know me. You know next to nothing about me. And now that you've—" she glanced meaningfully down at her naked body "—made your conquest…"

"Whoa." He was insulted.

"I'm not naive."

Okay, now he was the one getting angry. "This wasn't about a conquest, Darci."

She studied his expression. "I believe you believe that."

"And you think *I'm* cynical."

"It's not cynical to be realistic. Go to Paris and let your hormones calm down. Come back. If you still want to see me, you know where I'll be."

"Come here."

"Why?"

"Because you're talking like a crazy person. I want to remind you of what we've got."

"You mean lust?"

"Cynic." He crooked his finger and motioned her over.

She didn't move. "You'll leave my job alone. No more talk about me working for Tuck."

"If that's what you want. Then no more talk about Tuck."

"I mean it, Shane. No raises or promotions, either."

"You are so refreshing."

"I don't even know what that means."

"Most women beg me to help them."

"I'm not most women."

"No kidding. Now get over here. Bring your wine. You're staying in my arms for a while."

Eight

"So, did I just make the biggest mistake of my life?" Darci finished the story the next day, sitting at her computer across from Jennifer, in front of the reflective windows in the main room of their loft.

"Maybe not the biggest," said Jennifer as she dragged and clicked her mouse.

The two desks were identical and faced each other, allowing the women to work and talk at the same time. They'd skipped right through lunch, and she was hungry. But Darci was determined to finish setting up a series of photos for a high-end hotel chain before she called it a day.

"But it was big." She was trying hard to regret making love with Shane, but so far it wasn't working.

"Depends on how you look at it."

"I *made love* with Shane Colborn." There was only one way to look at it. Jennifer needed to tell her she'd been wrong.

"It might get you some additional snooping opportunities," said Jennifer, a meaningful expression on her face. "I mean, now that you've broken the ice."

"I didn't do it for that."

"I know you didn't."

"I wouldn't do it for that."

"But, you have to admit, it does open up some interesting possibilities. You might not have spent the night in his penthouse. But you could spend one in his mansion."

"I already decided not to." Darci had drawn herself an ethical line. She sincerely hoped she wouldn't cross it.

"You know where the records are now. It might get you there in one fell swoop."

"And if he catches me?"

Jennifer stopped working. "He's going to catch you, Darci. And if he doesn't catch you, you're going to find the drawings and tell him the truth. There's only one way this ends."

"I know."

"Do you?"

"I shouldn't have made love with him."

"Maybe not. But you did. And you're going to have to be tough about this. Think of it as a one-night stand."

"Right." Women had one-night stands. They did it all the time. Some of them did it with Shane Colborn.

"Have you never had a one-night stand?" asked Jennifer.

"You don't think I would have mentioned it?"

Jennifer gave a shrug. "I didn't."

The apparent confession shocked Darci. "*You* had a one-night stand?"

"Yes."

"With *who*?"

"With Ashton."

Darci waved the answer away. "Then it wasn't a one-night stand."

"It was at the time. It was the first night we met. I never thought I'd see him again."

A knock sounded on the apartment door.

Both women looked to the sound.

"Could it be Shane?" asked Jennifer in a hushed voice.

"He's on his way to France." Darci hesitated. "Unless."

Was she a fool to let her guard down? Half her secret was already out. Maybe he'd figured out the rest. Maybe he was angry enough to postpone the trip. Maybe this was the end.

"I'll talk to him," said Jennifer, rising from her chair. "You hide somewhere."

"I'm not climbing under the bed or cowering in the closet." If Darci was caught, she'd have to deal with it. She wasn't about to make the situation farcical.

"At least stand to one side," said Jennifer. "I'll tell him you're not here, buy you some time."

Darci moved from the line of sight.

The knock sounded again, and Jennifer went for the door.

Darci held her breath, bracing herself for Shane's angry voice.

"Ashton?" Jennifer's tone held obvious surprise.

Darci scrambled out from the corner.

"I only want to talk," said Ashton.

"Go away," Darci called.

But she was too late. Jennifer had opened the door to her ex.

"Back off, Darci," said Ashton.

"You need to leave her alone," said Darci, linking arms with Jennifer.

"It's okay," said Jennifer.

"This is not a good idea."

"I might as well get it over with," said Jennifer

"If you're sure," said Darci.

"I'm sure," said Jennifer. "But you stay, okay?"

Darci was thankful for small mercies. She reluctantly stepped aside.

Ashton closed the door behind him.

Nobody moved, and nobody said anything. The silence stretched to uncomfortable.

Ashton finally asked, "Can we sit down or something?"

"It's probably better if you just talk," said Darci, earning a glare from him.

Jennifer let out an exaggerated sigh. "Let's sit down." She looked at Darci. "A drink wouldn't be the worst idea in the world."

"Sure." Though Darci could use some fortification herself, she chafed at the idea of being hospitable to Ashton.

He took one end of the sofa, while Jennifer perched on the armchair across from him.

Darci went to the kitchen to hunt up some liquor.

"I know what you think you saw," Ashton opened.

"She was in your arms, Ashton. She was half-naked."

Darci's heart went out to Jennifer, and her annoyance at Ashton ramped up.

"*She* came on to *me*, he said."

"They always do," said Jennifer in an admirably even tone.

"Nothing happened," he said.

"Only because I showed up."

"No, not only because you showed up," he stated with conviction. "Nothing would have happened anyway."

"I guess we'll never know, will we?"

Darci forced herself to get to work on the drinks, taking three highball glasses from a top cupboard.

"One of us already knows," said Ashton. "Do you honestly think I'd sneak off into a bedroom in the middle of a party to cheat on you?"

"You thought I'd left."

Darci knew that Jennifer had left the party, ticked off at Ashton for flirting with the other woman. But Jennifer had forgotten her jacket and had come back to find the two of them together.

"I wasn't flirting," he said.

"Yes, you were. But that's not what set me over the edge."

"I was talking. Maybe she was flirting, but women do that all the time."

Jen scoffed out a laugh. "Because you're so irresistible?"

"I have no idea why they do it. I was coming after you, you know."

"By way of a bedroom?"

His tone went hard. "My jacket was in that bedroom. So was yours. So was everyone else's. If I was going to have sex with another woman, don't you think I would have picked somewhere with a little less traffic?"

Jennifer didn't answer immediately, and Darci opened the liquor cabinet and located a bottle of dark rum. Not her favorite, but she remembered Ashton hated rum. Maybe it would hurry him on his way.

"How am I supposed to know what you'd do?" asked Jennifer.

"She followed me into the bedroom. Then she pulled off her top."

Darci turned to the fridge and extracted a bottle of lemon-lime soda and a jug of orange juice.

"Next thing I knew, she was kissing me," said Ashton. "If you'd watched for another five seconds, you'd have seen me push her away."

"I was afraid to watch for another five seconds," said Jennifer.

Darci knew in her heart he had to be lying, but he came across as sincere. She could only hope that Jennifer wasn't being swayed.

She added ice cubes to the drinks and carried two of the glasses into the living room.

Ashton frowned at the drink.

"Rum punch," said Darci.

Jennifer hid an involuntary smile and took a sip. "Yum."

"Thanks." Ashton's voice was flat.

Darci ignored the tone. "No problem."

She returned to the kitchen to retrieve her own drink.

"You hounded me for three weeks to say *that*?" asked Jennifer.

Darci was heartened by the skepticism in her tone.

"It's the truth," said Ashton, again managing an impressive level of sincerity.

"I don't believe you," said Jennifer.

"I know." He took a drink of the punch and grimaced. "But I had to try."

Darci returned to the living area, quietly taking the opposite end of the sofa. She knew she shouldn't be here for this intimate conversation, but she was afraid to leave Jennifer alone with him.

Silence stretched again.

"I'm sorry," said Jennifer.

Darci wanted to ask why. But she took a sip of the drink instead. She grimaced. It was terrible.

"You don't need to be sorry," Ashton said to Jennifer. "I completely understand why you reacted the way you did. I don't blame you. In your shoes, I'd have thought the same thing. Of course, I'd have taken the guy's head off."

Despite herself, Darci felt her sympathies engage with Ashton. He looked sincerely wounded. Jennifer's expression relaxed, as well, her eyes softening.

Uh-oh. This was how he did it every time.

"You'd never find her in that situation," said Darci, overwhelmed by the urge to defend her friend.

Ashton sent her a dark look.

"This is how he does it. He puts on that hurt-puppy-dog look, tells you he understands your feelings, that it was circumstances that conspired against him, and you're right back on the merry-go-round."

"It's different," said Ashton.

Darci struggled not to speak. She sat back and took a big swallow of her drink. It didn't taste so bad this time.

"You better go," said Jennifer. "I listened…but you better go."

Ashton frowned.

"Please," said Jennifer.

"I can't."

"You have to."

He polished off the drink and rose from the couch. "I didn't do it. I wouldn't do it. I'm not perfect, but I wouldn't hurt you like that."

Darci rose. "Let her go," she told him.

"It's different," Ashton said to Jennifer. "You're different. Or maybe I'm different."

"I can't," she said, her voice cracking.

"I get that now. And I know it's all my fault." He pivoted and crossed the room.

As the door slammed shut behind him, Jennifer's shoulders slumped.

"Are you okay?" Darci asked.

"Does that scare you?" Jennifer asked. "It should scare you."

"Me?"

"I've been talking too tough."

"With Ashton?" Darci struggled to understand.

"With Shane. I've been giving you this flip, simplistic advice for dealing with Shane, ignoring how your emotions might get muddled up. And now you're wandering into danger."

"I'm not—"

"You *are*."

Darci sat back down. Things were complicated with Shane, for sure. But dangerous?

"You are absolutely going to betray him," said Jennifer. "There'll be no ambiguity, and he's going to know you did it."

It wasn't the same. It wasn't anywhere near the same.

"He'll hate you for it," said Jennifer. "And that could break your heart."

"My heart's not involved."

Jennifer leaned forward. "And if that changes?"

"It never will. And Shane hasn't fallen for me."

"You better hope not."

Darci didn't have to hope. It was never going to happen. She at least had that going for her.

"I hear you've come over to the dark side," said Tuck as he pulled back a chair in Daelan's Bar and Grill.

Just back from France Thursday evening, Shane was sipping his second beer and working his way through a slice of deep-dish pizza. He'd been up for nearly twenty hours.

"I convinced him to try out a Gulfstream," said Justin.

"Go big or go home," said Tuck as he helped himself to a slice of the sausage-and-mushroom special.

The waitress quickly arrived with Tuck's favorite beer.

"Thank you, darlin'," said Tuck, accepting the frosted mug. "How'd it go?" he asked Shane.

"Did you know Darci works for me?" Shane returned.

It hadn't gone particularly well in France. Riley Ellis had come up again as a potential competitor, and Shane was beginning to wonder if he'd underestimated both the man and Ellis Air. But right now he wanted to find out what Tuck had known about Darci.

"No kidding," said Tuck. "That's weird."

"Did you know?"

"How would I know?"

"She's your friend."

"No, she's—" Tuck seemed to catch himself. "We're acquaintances. I thought she had her own business."

Shane couldn't shake a nagging suspicion that Tuck knew

more than he was saying. "She does." He watched his friend carefully. "But she also works for Colborn."

"Small world," Tuck said easily. "Is that why she was at your party?"

"She crashed the party."

Tuck chuckled, not looking like a man harboring some deep, dark secret. "You should get more security. Or less security, if that's the kind of woman who's going to crash your parties."

Shane made the decision to set aside his suspicions. Whatever was bothering his gut about the situation, it didn't seem to be connected to Tuck. "That's why she didn't want to sleep with me."

"He's obsessed about that," said Justin. "He simply can't fathom that a woman would say no to him based on good taste alone."

"I don't care if she says no. I don't care if any woman says no. It's the mixed signals that were killing me."

"Are the signals now unmixed?" asked Tuck.

Shane hesitated. He didn't intend to kiss and tell. "She's worried about having a relationship with the boss."

"Smart woman," said Justin.

Tuck smirked. "So, she's available?"

"Back off," Shane ordered, his suspicions coming back in full force.

"Chill," said Tuck, taking a swig of his beer. "I swear I'll keep my hands off Darci."

Deep down, Shane knew he could trust Tuck. "I need you to do me a favor."

"Sure." Tuck bit into his pizza.

"I haven't worked out the kinks yet, so don't you say anything to her. I just want to know it's an option."

Tuck nodded. "What do you need?"

"Offer Darci a job at Tucker Transportation."

"Nice solution," said Justin, giving his beer mug a little raise.

"No problem," said Tuck. "Do you have a copy of her resume?"

"I can pull it for you," replied Justin.

"Then consider it done."

"I still have to convince her to take it," said Shane.

"Could be she wants an excuse to stay out of your bed," said Justin.

"That's not it," spat Shane. He instantly realized he'd said too much, and he directed his attention to his pizza.

"Just keep it out of the headlines," Justin muttered.

"She's not that kind of girl."

His two friends waited in silence, but Shane didn't offer anything more. Darci didn't deserve to be office gossip or any other kind.

The sooner he got her settled in a job *away* from Colborn, the better.

"Stay," Shane's deep voice intoned in Darci's ear.

They'd had dinner together on the deck of his penthouse but had quickly ended up in his bed.

She'd told herself a two-night stand was no worse than a one-night stand, and she almost believed it.

She'd also told herself she could have a physical relationship with Shane while keeping her emotions out of the mix.

"That's not a good idea," she told him.

"Why?"

"Because…" *I'm lying to you.* "We're only just getting to know each other."

"I'm handsome, successful and good in bed. What else do you need to know?"

She tried not to laugh. "It's not twenty questions."

"Tell me about your family. I feel I'm at a disadvantage since you know so much about mine."

She realized she'd walked into a minefield. "It was just me and my dad." She chose her words carefully. "Our apartment was small, but we were close to a park with an outdoor rink. I liked skating."

"Were you good?"

"I was okay. What about you? Any sports in your past?"

"Second base."

"Were you good?"

"For a high school kid. Tuck and I liked parties."

"He told me."

"He did?"

"He said you both had fancy cars and got into nightclubs."

"That was when we were older," said Shane. "In high school, we had parties at the beach."

"Girls in bikinis?"

"As often as possible."

"Were you a spoiled rich kid?"

"I was privileged. There's no getting around that. And high school was a blast. But then…my parents were killed. And everything changed."

She felt her sympathies engage. "Tuck told me that, too."

"I'm trying hard not to be jealous of Tuck."

"What happened with your parents?"

"They were in a speedboat, one of my dad's hobbies. They hit something on the water and flipped going about sixty knots. I was on shore. It was a bad day."

"I'm so sorry."

Her feelings for Dalton Colborn didn't matter. It was a human tragedy, something Shane had had to cope with at far too young an age.

"Things got rocky with the company for a couple of years after that."

"Did you have help?" she asked. "Were there people in the company who were experienced and supportive?"

"Justin's been great throughout." He looped an arm around her shoulders. "Why are we talking about this? It was a long time ago."

"It's part of who you are."

"I want to talk about you."

"I'm dull by comparison."

"I don't believe that for one second." He brushed a kiss

against her hairline. "Stay. Sleep with me. Wake up with me tomorrow morning, eat waffles…relax. Maybe tell me your secrets."

She fought a rising anxiety. "You know it's too complicated."

He sat up, his bare torso gleaming in the moonlight. "Let me make it simple."

"You can't make it simple."

The only person who could make it simple was Darci. And that happened only if she walked away from everything, including Shane, her search and her growing feelings.

He took her hand in both of his. "Let me try. Now, here's the thing, Tuck says he can easily give you a job."

She sat up. "You talked to Tuck about this?"

"Yes."

Embarrassment overwhelmed her. "You told him what's going on?"

"I told him that you work for me. That I like you, and I want to pursue something."

"Did you tell him we were having sex?"

"*No.* We're not having sex. I mean, it's not like that."

She knew what he was trying to say. But she also knew the truth. It wasn't like that. It was far worse than that.

In a flash, Darci realized she couldn't keep up the deception. She was mortified she'd let it get this far. She was betraying him horribly. She had to come clean, to tell him the truth. No matter how ugly it got, anything had to be better than this.

She turned to brace her feet on the floor, framing up the words in her head, gathering her courage, trying desperately not to think about how bad this could go.

She fisted one hand around the comforter and opened her mouth. But his cell phone rang on the bedside table.

She moaned under her breath, her courage deserting her.

"I'm ignoring it," he said.

"Get it." She flipped back the covers and rose from the bed. The phone call was nowhere near to being her biggest problem.

"Darci, wait."

"I'll be right back." She scooped up his white dress shirt and draped it over her shoulders, heading for the en suite bathroom.

"Yeah?" she heard him say into the phone.

She gripped the edge of the counter and stared into the vanity mirror. She had to make her choice. Right here, right now. She could either sleep with Shane or lie to him. She couldn't live with herself if she did both.

Shane or her father? It had to be her father. He was her family. That was her loyalty.

But that meant ending it with Shane. She had to get dressed, walk out the door and never hold him again.

How could she bring herself to do that?

"How?" Shane asked sharply into the phone.

She glanced over her shoulder. Had the Beaumont deal gone bad?

Shane was sitting on the opposite edge of the bed, his back to her, shoulders rigid.

"Are you *sure*?" he asked, his tone ice-cold. "Absolutely 100 percent?"

Her heart went out to him. Colborn might be a massive corporation, but she knew they'd overextended themselves recently on research and development. Losing both Gobrecht and Beaumont would put them in serious financial trouble.

It occurred to her that she should be satisfied, glad even, that the Colborn empire had ended up this way. It served Dalton Colborn right. But she couldn't bring herself to wish Shane any harm.

She stared at her reflection in the mirror. She had to tell him. She was going to tell him.

"You have exactly ten seconds," said Shane, appearing in the bathroom doorway, a pair of gray sweatpants clinging low on his hips.

She took in his steely glare. Did he mean, to take the job with Tuck? He'd give her an ultimatum like that?

"To explain why Darci *Rivers* is sleeping with Shane Colborn."

A cold wave washed through her, and she lost all feeling in her knees.

He waited, but she couldn't speak. There was a roar building inside her head. She couldn't form a thought, never mind a coherent sentence.

"Gotta give you credit for commitment," he drawled, his gaze running from her disheveled hair to her bare legs. "Talk about above and beyond."

She quickly closed the gaping shirt front.

"A little late for modesty."

She found her voice. "How did you—?"

"It doesn't matter *how*. You lying, little—"

"I didn't mean to—"

"Didn't mean to what?" He took a slow step forward. "Didn't mean to lie to me?"

"Yes. No. I *did* mean to lie to you. Of course I meant to lie to you." She scrambled to put her thoughts in order. "I never thought I'd meet you in person."

"You were in my house. You work at my business."

"Only temporarily. I needed…to find something." How was she going to explain? And if she did, wouldn't he immediately destroy the evidence?

She swallowed.

"Your father's fabled drawings," said Shane with cold, clipped precision.

Darci staggered back. "You have my father's drawings?"

"There *are* no drawings."

She was too late. The Colborns had found the drawings. They'd destroyed them, and her father's genius would never be known.

"Did you burn them?"

His head snapped back. "What? No. We didn't burn them. They never existed."

"Right. Sure. Whatever."

It was too much to hope that he'd be honest. She moved to go past him. She needed to get dressed and get out of here.

He didn't stop her, turning as she passed by him and went into the bedroom.

"Your father made that story up, Darci. He was after a payout."

She kept walking away. "I should have known."

"That he made it up?"

"No." She should have known the Colborns would have covered their tracks. They were cunning, scheming billionaires.

"Should have known what?" he asked.

She gave a cold laugh as she hunted for her underwear. How much more humiliating could this get? "That your family would have long since destroyed the evidence. I'm hopelessly outclassed."

"There was no evidence to destroy."

"Of course there wasn't." Sarcasm dripped from her words.

Forget the underwear. She dropped his shirt on the floor and quickly pulled her dress over her naked body.

She turned to face him. "There's no need to fire me. I quit."

"You're not... Yeah, I guess you are fired. Exactly how long have you been working for me?"

"Less than a month."

"So, right before the party?"

She closed her eyes, then opened them, heaving a sigh. "You won, okay. You won, and I lost."

"So, the wine cellar, the earring, all of that was about getting into the records storage?"

"*I found the right boxes,*" she challenged. "But I couldn't get back there to look through them."

"And the dogs?"

She shuddered at the memory.

"Were you ever afraid of dogs? Or was that a lie, too?"

"I am afraid of dogs. Lots of things weren't lies, Shane." Their gazes met.

"It's why you asked about the security system," he said.

"You volunteered that. I wasn't about to break into your

mansion, Shane. I was just…" As she spoke, her guilt ramped up. "You know, poking around."

"You took the job so you could poke around corporate headquarters."

"I did."

"And you dated me to get inside the mansion."

She flinched at that one.

His glance went to the disheveled bed. "You really are a piece of work."

"I didn't sleep with you to get the information. I tried *not* to sleep with you."

His voice went low. "You can't have it both ways, Darci."

"I know. I figured that out. This was a really, really big mistake."

Her heart was starting to ache.

"You believe it, don't you?" he asked.

"That this was a mistake?" She believed that with every fiber of her being.

"That Colborn is hiding your father's original drawings for the turbine."

"No. I believe Colborn destroyed the drawings for my father's turbine."

"Why would we do that?"

She scoffed out a laugh. "For the money, Shane."

"We have plenty of money. We'd share it if you were legally entitled."

"Right." Darci didn't believe that for a second.

"Your father lied," said Shane. "Or else he was delusional. He drank, didn't he?"

"Don't you *dare*! On top of everything else, don't make my father out to be a crazy drunk." She paused. "Or is that your defense strategy?"

"I don't need a defense strategy."

"Of course, you don't. You destroyed all the proof. Did you burn it? Shred it? Toss it into the ocean? Thank goodness it happened before the boom in scanners. Who knows how many copies you might have been forced to track down."

"He was jealous," said Shane. "If he hadn't walked away from the company…"

"You mean if Dalton hadn't walked away with my father's intellectual property."

The silence swelled around them.

"He convinced you completely, didn't he?" asked Shane.

"He never said a word. I only found out accidentally, after he died three months ago."

The room went silent again.

She told herself to move, but nothing happened.

After a few minutes, Shane gave a nod. "Okay. If you're so sure. If you think the drawings exist, have at it."

"Have at what?"

"Have at my basement. Have at my office. Check the vault. I'll let you look anywhere you want."

Darci searched his expression, trying to see what the catch was. Obviously, he thought all the evidence had been destroyed. But her father had seemed certain something would have survived. Maybe there was something Shane didn't know about.

"We can do it right now," said Shane. "We'll go to the mansion this very minute, look through it before I have a chance to tamper with the records room."

It seemed too good to be true.

"Why would you do that?" she asked with suspicion.

"Because I'm not a liar." He reached out to her.

She quickly backed away. "Don't."

He let his hand drop and asked, "Why couldn't you have been what you seemed?"

Her chest went tight with remorse.

"Why can't any woman be what she seems?" he asked under his breath.

She blinked hard, battling her misery, turning away to find the rest of her belongings.

Nine

The wine cellar turned out to be the most convenient space to go through the records. It wouldn't have been Shane's first choice. It brought back too many memories of that first evening with Darci. But it was close to the records room, had comfortable chairs and a big table, where Darci was already sorting pages into piles.

On the phone with Justin, Shane stopped just inside the cellar, standing to one side while Ben unloaded another ten boxes from the trolley.

"From a legal standpoint," said Justin, "there's no severance required if the layoffs are due to a lack of work. You only need two weeks' notice."

"I don't want layoffs at all." Clearly Shane wasn't making his point. "Can we not redeploy employees?"

"To where?"

"I came up with an idea," said Shane. "Accounting and operations say that if the Gobrecht contract is gone, we have a one-year gap where we only require fifty percent staffing levels."

"Hence, the need for layoffs."

Shane pulled out a chair at the far end of the table from Darci. "I'm putting together a scenario where we build forty jets for the private market, a scaled-down version of the Aware 200. With the rise in Asian economies, that segment of the market is growing. We can offer competitive fuel economy with a higher top speed, perfect for transpacific travel."

"You have buyers already?"

"On spec."

There was a brief pause. "I'm sorry. I couldn't have heard that right. You said on spec?"

"Yes." Shane knew it was a financial risk, but it was a calculated financial risk.

"Forty jets *on spec*?"

"I think you heard me the first two times."

"You'll *bankrupt the company.*"

"Calm down. I'm not going to bankrupt us."

Darci glanced up.

Shane gave a reflexive smile before he remembered he was royally ticked off at her. He glanced away but was still hyper-aware of her presence.

"You can't do that Shane."

"We're running the numbers now. Yes, it'll be expensive."

"That's an understatement. Who in their right mind would finance it?"

"We've got plenty of collateral."

"You're not actually saying this. We are not having this conversation."

"Justin—"

"No, Shane. I can't let you do it. If half your people get laid off, they get laid off. That's how it works in the real world. Hopefully, new contracts come, and you hire them back. But if you gamble and lose, there's no company to hire them back into, and everybody else loses their jobs, as well. You're not doing them any favors, Shane."

"I am if we sell the private jets. They'll take two years to build. We can probably sell some while they're in production, and the rest will be shipment ready." Shane could feel Darci's gaze on him again.

"And if you don't?" asked Justin.

"We will."

"This isn't how you run a business."

"It's how *I* run a business. We'll beef up the sales team, put our R & D section to work. The Colborn engine will be the cornerstone, saving clients' time and fuel costs. But we can also incorporate technology into the cabins, connectivity, full-office functionality in the seats, more comfortable sleeping options, better galley space." Comfort and convenience were the way of the future.

"It's a brand-new market for you."

"Tuck and Dixon have helped me see the light." An inspiration hit him. "Dixon will help our sales force get started. The man's got connections all over the world. There are more people like me out there, Justin, people who've never considered a private jet and don't know what they're missing."

Darci made an inarticulate sound. It could have been a cough, or it could have been a laugh.

Shane couldn't stop himself from looking at her.

Her brows were raised in obvious incredulity.

He covered the phone. "There are plenty of corporations who can afford a jet."

"Plenty," she mocked.

"You're going to roll the dice," said Justin.

"I'm not going to lay off eight hundred workers. It's in our interest to keep them. Some of them have very specific skill sets."

"Let me go over your corporate structure."

"Sure."

"We can at least protect the mansion."

Shane chuckled. "If I lose Colborn, I won't be able to afford the mansion."

"This isn't a joke."

"Who's laughing?"

"You are."

"Fair point," said Shane.

"I'm coming over."

"Not tonight." Then Shane rethought that position. "On second thought, do come over tonight."

He could use the moral support, and he could use the distraction. Because it didn't seem to matter that Darci had lied to him, betrayed him and was going after Colborn, she still looked gorgeous, sitting here in the wine cellar, meticulously reading through paper after paper. In his eyes, she was still the sexiest woman alive, and he didn't want to make a fool of himself by making a pass at her.

"I'll be there in an hour." Justin signed off.

Shane pocketed his phone.

For a few minutes, Darci silently sorted papers.

"Are you thirsty?" he asked her.

"I'm fine."

He rose. "Well, I'm thirsty." He wasn't about to sit down here craving a drink.

"Is your new strategy because of the Beaumont contract?" she asked.

"Not entirely." He decided to go for something French. "Beaumont is still in play, but without Gobrecht, we'll have to shut down one of our production facilities. I want to re-purpose it to make smaller jets aimed at the private market."

"You can't find a replacement contract?"

"Not fast enough." He drew out a bottle. "And I really liked the private jet."

"Imagine that."

He gave an involuntary smile. "Not just from a luxury per-spective, though that was top-notch. The Colborn engine can offer time and fuel savings, and we'll meet, if not better, the cabin comforts of other manufacturers."

"Is this because you want a private jet?"

"That's where it started. The first one definitely goes to me."

He decided against the Beaujolais and moved on.

"You could just build the one."

He shook his head, moving along the racks. "Not remotely cost effective."

"You could buy one from another company."

"I could. But then eight hundred workers won't have jobs."

She continued sorting while he checked out a dusty bottle of Bordeaux.

"Just how risky is this?" she asked.

"Are you asking for youself?"

She looked puzzled.

"You're worried about your theoretical, prospective finan-cial windfall?"

There was a beat before she answered. "Yes. That's it ex-actly."

"The risk is pretty huge. But, you know what? I've never

put my stamp on this company. My dad conceived and built it, and I've pretty much been the caretaker since he died."

"Does that bother you?" she asked, her tone more curious than cutting.

"I wouldn't have said so yesterday. But I think it does." He brushed the dust off another label.

"Did you have a good relationship with your father?"

"It was fine. You probably don't want to hear that, since he's the villain in your little scenario."

"My little scenario? Otherwise known as the truth?"

He ignored her sarcasm. "We weren't best buddies or anything. He was serious and hardworking. We had a shared interest in aerospace, and he taught me most of what I know about business."

"Would he save eight hundred jobs?"

Shane doubted it. "There's no way to know."

"I think you do know." Her gaze was perceptive enough to be disconcerting.

"All I know is that I'm going to try."

"You're not your father."

"You never met my father."

She seemed to realize she'd stopped sorting through the files. She turned her attention to the box in front of her.

"Find anything damning?" he asked.

"I'm on box one of fifty."

He looked at the label of the bottle in his hand. It was Chateau Marcess, one of his father's particular favorites.

He was struck by the irony but carried the bottle to the tasting table anyway. While Darci stayed focused on the files, he popped the cork and poured two glasses of the Bordeaux.

"Tell me about your father," he said, taking the chair around the corner from her and sliding a glass her way.

"He was great," she responded without looking up.

"Great?"

"Yes."

Shane swirled the wine in the glass to help aerate the wine, then took a first sip. "What was great about him?"

She leaned forward to place a paper on one of about ten stacks she had going. "These files are a mess."

"They're forty years old."

"Nobody knew the alphabet back then?"

Something seemed to catch her eye. As she lifted the page, Shane realized it was a photograph. She angled it to catch the light and stared.

"Who is it?" he asked.

"My dad. And I'm guessing yours, too." She handed the photo over to him.

The two men stood in front of a cinder block warehouse with a distinctive, powder blue garage-type door. Shane recognized it as the D&I facility. They were arm in arm, goofy grins on their faces. They must have only been in their early twenties, and their long hair looked ridiculous.

"Simpler times," said Shane.

"They look really happy." Darci absently lifted her glass of wine and took a drink.

"They were."

"Do you know what happened between them?" she asked.

He didn't know much. "Your mom left. Your dad got depressed and lost interest in working. So they shut down the company."

Her brow furrowed. "Is that how you heard it?"

"How did you hear it?"

It took her a minute to answer. "I didn't. At least, nothing specific until I found a letter he'd written but never mailed. While I was growing up, my dad would rant whenever he came across the Colborn name. To him, Dalton was the devil incarnate."

"Sour grapes?" asked Shane.

"Victim of betrayal," she responded and went back to sorting records.

Shane lifted another file box onto the table and flipped open the lid.

"What are you doing?" she asked.

"Searching for evidence."

Her expression faltered.

"It's a double-edged sword," he said. "There's an equal chance that what's in these boxes will disprove your theory as prove it."

"No, there's not," she said.

He couldn't help but smile. "I admire your confidence."

"I know my father. My mother leaving didn't make him depressed. It was your father's betrayal that did that."

"You never told me why he was great."

"You don't care. You don't really want to know."

"Yes, I do."

She looked him square in the eye. "Why?"

"Because he inspired your loyalty."

"He was my father."

"It's beyond that. You've embarked on a life of crime. You lied. You stole. You *slept* with me."

"I didn't steal anything."

"You were trying."

She didn't seem to have an answer to that. But she did take another sip of wine.

"What kind of man inspires a woman to take such enormous risks?"

Even as he asked, Shane realized he barely knew Darci. And what he did know about her was entirely fabricated.

"He raised me," she said. "My mother walked out, and he didn't. He might not have had a lot of money, but he made sure I had clothes and food and a roof over my head. He read to me at night, and stood in the cold while I skated. He might have even been battling depression, but he stuck it out to take care of me."

"Where did you grow up?" Shane felt a twist of guilt over their vastly different upbringings. Not that it was his fault, or his father's fault, for that matter.

"The South Side. The neighborhood wasn't bad, mostly single-parent families." She pursed her lips in defiance.

"I'm sure it was fine."

"No private school and rowing team."

"You got into Columbia. Or was that a lie, too?"

"It *wasn't* a lie."

"Glad to hear it."

"I wouldn't lie about that."

He lifted his brow. "Really?"

"I only lied where I had to lie. And even then it was for the greater good."

"The greater good being money?"

"The greater good being justice and the restoration of my father's professional name."

"And money. You do know this would mean a whole lot of money."

She went back to sorting. "I don't care about that."

"Forgive me if I'm skeptical."

"Listen, Shane." She knocked the side of her fist against the solid tabletop. "If there's any money coming to my family, it was earned and justified. I'm not going to apologize for that."

"You've got a big family to share it with, do you?"

She glared at him.

He couldn't bring himself to believe she was a con artist, but he also couldn't let his personal feelings color his judgment. The woman had lied to him from minute one. She was definitely trying to get her hooks into Colborn Aerospace. And he couldn't let her big green eyes, pouty lips and those perfect breasts make him stupid.

Darci knew Shane didn't trust her. That was fine. He didn't need to trust her. He only needed to let her keep looking through the company records.

She wished he'd leave her alone to do just that. Having him in the wine cellar with her was an incessant reminder of what could never be. Jennifer had been right all along. This was the only way it could ever end.

Darci had known sleeping with him was fraught with risk. But she hadn't expected all-out heartache. She hadn't expected to feel this desolate when it all came to a close. It had only been a few hours, and already she missed every little thing about him.

Justin appeared in the doorway of the wine cellar, his attention instantly zeroing in on the files and the boxes.

"What the—?" he asked, his gaze shooting to Shane, then to Darci, then back again.

"Hi, Justin," said Shane.

She arched a brow at Shane. "He didn't know I was here?"

"Why would he know you were here?"

"What is *going on*?" Justin demanded.

"We're looking through the historical files," said Shane.

"Have you lost your mind? I mean, more than once today? Did I not tell you she was Darci Rivers?"

"You did."

"Her father was a paranoid lunatic."

"Excuse me?" said Darci.

Justin ignored her. "She's been lying to you for weeks. You're giving her access to the original files? Who knows what she'll do. She could destroy something, or plant something."

Shane looked at her. "Darci, are you going to plant fake documents in the Colborn files?"

"Do you want to search my purse?" she asked. "Maybe put me up against the wall and frisk me?"

His pupils dilated, and his nostrils flared.

It was a stupid, inflammatory thing to say, but she didn't care.

"She didn't say no," Justin pointed out.

"No," said Darci. "I'm not planting anything in the files. I'm looking for the truth. That's all I've ever been doing."

"The truth is your father was either a liar or delusional."

"Justin," Shane warned. "There's no point in bickering our way through fifty boxes of files."

"You'd be foolish to leave her alone with them," warned Justin.

"I'm not leaving you two alone with them, either," she responded.

If they hadn't already destroyed her father's evidence, she sure wasn't giving them a shot at it now.

Justin gave a laugh of disbelief, obviously questioning her power to do anything about it.

But she did have power. She folded her arms across her chest. "How would you feel about a brand-new tell-all book written by the daughter of the man Colborn Aerospace defrauded?"

"That's absurd," said Justin. "We'd sue you for libel. Your ass would be inside a courtroom so fast."

"Justin!" shouted Shane.

"We'd prove she was lying."

"Like we proved Bianca was lying?"

"That's an entirely different—"

"It's exactly the same," said Shane. Then he turned on Darci, his eyes cold. "You'd do that?"

"In a heartbeat." She doubted she'd be able to go through with it. But she loved her dad. There wasn't anything she wouldn't do for him or his memory.

"So, what do you propose?" asked Shane.

It was a good question. "We look together. You don't trust me. I don't trust you."

"24-7?"

It was a valid question. The second she went home, Shane and Justin would have unfettered access to the files. They could burn the whole lot of them if they wanted.

"It's the only arrangement that works," she allowed.

"Which means you're staying?"

She really hadn't thought this through. "I'm not sleeping with you."

He gave a cool smirk. "I'm offering a guest room."

She glanced around at the boxes, wondering how long it would take her to get through them all. One day? Two days?

"How committed are you?" Shane's tone was soft and taunting.

"Completely committed." She glared at him in defiance.

"I'll stay as long as it takes. It's not like I have a job to go back to."

"I fired her," Shane told Justin.

"I quit," Darci corrected.

"Why are you indulging her?" asked Justin.

"She thinks she's right."

Darci bristled. "I *am* right."

"Then why the elaborate ruse?" Justin asked her. "Why not just knock on the front door?"

She counted off on her fingers. "Because I'm not stupid. Because it would have tipped you off. Because Dalton swindled my father. Because Colborns can't be trusted."

"Reverse the roles," Shane said to Justin. "If you were her, what would you do?"

"Your judgment is clouded. You're taking an unnecessary risk."

"Maybe. But at this point, it doesn't matter. Another tell-all book would completely destroy us."

"You should never have—" Justin didn't finish the sentence. He didn't need to.

Mortification swept over Darci.

In Justin's mind, she was no better than Bianca. And Shane had to feel the same. She realized that if she didn't find her father's drawings, it was always going to look that way to him.

She swallowed against a lump of regret. She couldn't let herself care about Shane's opinion. She had to focus on finding the designs for her father's sake. If she failed, she failed. But she had to give it her all.

"We need a break," said Shane. "Let's go upstairs and figure out how this is going to work."

Darci glanced at her watch. It was nearly ten o'clock at night.

She came to her feet. "I have to call Jennifer."

Justin left first while Shane waited for Darci to move toward the door.

"Maybe she can bring you some underwear," he muttered as she passed.

She twisted to shoot him a glare. But when she met his eyes, a surge of sexual awareness shuddered through her body. She was completely naked beneath her dress, and they both knew it.

"Don't," she hissed.

"Don't what?"

"No sexual innuendo."

"Not talking won't make us stop thinking."

"This isn't going to work if you taunt me."

"This isn't going to work anyway."

Darci wished she could tell him he was wrong. But he wasn't. Being cooped up with Shane for however long it took to go through fifty boxes of records was going to be excruciating.

Darci dropped box twenty-six onto the floor of the wine cellar with a clunk. So far, she'd found absolutely nothing to indicate her father's invention had been stolen.

Shane had long since stopped looking through the historical records, instead turning the wine cellar into a makeshift office. It was Wednesday, and a steady parade of staff had been marching in and out, providing information and advice while he dealt with dozens of issues, from aviation regulations and flight tests to robotic equipment glitches and staff training.

He spent the majority of his time with Justin, working on either the Beaumont contract or the planned changeover to produce private jets. The two men had spirited discussions, either forgetting Darci was at the other end of the table or deciding she wouldn't be able to do anything with the corporate information anyway.

Every time Justin suggested they scale down the Colborn operations, Shane stood his ground. She couldn't help but be proud of his convictions. He didn't seem willing to lay off a single employee.

"Riley Ellis again," said Justin as he entered the cellar, pulling out a chair to park himself across the table from Shane.

"What now?" asked Shane. "What is *with* that guy?"

"He's headhunting your employees."

"Which ones?"

"Technicians, mostly, but also engineers. He's offering salary bumps, more holidays and better benefits."

"How can he afford it? And, really, what the hell? Last time I looked, he was a hundred-man operation. And now he's bidding competitively on international contracts?"

"He's gone into partnership with Zavier Tac."

"Why?"

"To compete on international contracts," said Justin.

"I mean why would Zavier Tac work with Ellis? What's in it for them?"

"I don't know. I'll try to find out."

"Okay," said Shane. "And find out what it's going to take to keep our guys?"

"You can't keep them."

"What do you mean, I can't keep them? I have to keep them. It's not like we can replace them."

"If you bump their pay, you have to bump the pay of the entire employment class. The cost is way too high."

Shane spat out a pithy swearword. Then he glanced at Darci. "Sorry."

"Offer lunch," she suggested.

"Excuse me?"

"I know it's not a problem at your head office, so you probably haven't paid attention. But at the assembly and manufacturing plants, there's nowhere for employees to go out for lunch."

"We have cafeterias," said Justin.

"And they're subsidized," said Shane.

"Exactly. So it wouldn't cost much to make lunch completely free. Revamp the menu to offer restaurant-quality food, more variety. Throw in some recreation equipment. I don't know—Ping-Pong tables, maybe a basketball court and video games."

"Have you lost your—?"

"Let her talk," said Shane.

"Make your employees feel valued beyond their paychecks. Lunch was the number-one issue around the water cooler.

Form an employee committee to design the new menus and make the recreational plans. You could do that as early as tomorrow morning."

"Why are you suggesting this?" asked Shane.

"I don't know." She honestly didn't know what had given her this urge to help out. "You two seem so pathetic over there, trying to run such a big company all on your own."

Justin rolled his eyes, but Shane clearly fought a grin.

"It's not the worst idea in the world," said Shane.

"There's gotta be a catch," said Justin, watching her with suspicion.

"I'm planning on stopping by for the free lunch," she said.

"You're not on our side," said Justin.

"I'm on the side of Colborn Aerospace." She refused to admit she was losing hope of finding anything to substantiate her father's claim. "And somewhere in these last twenty-four boxes is the proof I need to get my piece of the pie."

"At least that makes sense," said Justin.

"Do it," said Shane. "Talk to the plant managers, and announce it tomorrow."

"Uh-oh," came a voice from the corner of the room.

They all looked at David, one of Shane's assistants who'd been in and out over the past few days.

David glanced up from where he'd been talking on his phone. "It's Bianca. She went on with Berkley Nash again."

"Somebody kill me," said Shane, dropping his chin to his chest. "Just get a gun and end it now."

"What did she say?" asked Justin.

"Don't tell me." Shane held up his hands to forestall David. "I'm not wasting any more time on that woman. Go over the video tonight, jot down only what I absolutely need to know and bring it to me in the morning."

"Yes, sir." David came to his feet.

Justin stood, as well. "I'll ride back to the city with you," he said to David.

"Call me with the free-lunch details," said Shane as they left the room.

Darci knew she had to toughen up, but her heart went out to Shane. She'd been watching him work like a madman for three days now. He seemed to be trying valiantly to do the right thing, and he was getting whacked with problems from all sides.

"You okay?" she asked in the now silent room.

He twisted around to look down the length of the table at her. "Not really."

"I don't much like Bianca Covington."

"Neither do I." His gaze seemed to soften. "And I don't much like fighting with you."

"It's hard not to fight when we're on opposite sides."

He gave a sad smile. "I wish you were on my side."

"And I wish you were on mine." It would be so much nicer if Shane was trying to find the real truth instead of trying to protect his family.

They gazed at each other.

She wished she could go to him. She wished she could stand up, walk the length of this table and hold him close. She'd tell him it was going to be all right. And he'd tell her the same thing. And then they'd find a way to make it all right together.

Shane's phone rang.

He frowned as he reached for it. "Yeah?"

He broke the gaze. "What? Are you sure?" He raked a hand through his hair. "She's lying. She's flat-out lying."

He came to his feet, pacing toward the wall. He stopped and smacked his fist on the stone. "That'll be the ballgame then." He paused. "Yeah." Another pause. "Tomorrow."

He punched the off button with this thumb. Then he swore and drew his arm back. She thought he was going to hurl his phone across the room.

"Shane?" she ventured, standing.

He didn't answer, but he did turn to face her.

"Beaumont?" she dared ask.

"They saw the Bianca interview."

"Have they canceled?"

"We expect it in the morning."

"What could she have said? Never mind." Darci knew it was none of her business. "It doesn't matter. Whatever it was, it obviously destroyed your professional reputation. And it's hard to get that back."

"Are you mocking me?" he asked.

"What?" She was confused.

"Are you pointing out the irony that you think my father destroyed your father, and karma's a bitch?"

"I never said that." She hadn't thought it, either.

She might have once, but right now, she simply felt sympathy for Shane. He didn't deserve what Bianca was doing. There was nothing karmic about it.

It was plain mean-spirited and grossly unfair. She was seized by another urge to help out.

And then she had an idea.

It was radical, and it was probably stupid. But she was in a unique position to comment publicly on Shane Colborn. She had a salacious angle, and she had little left to lose.

Ten

Halfway through the morning on Thursday, Darci disappeared from the wine cellar. Shane was surprised, since she'd been so adamant about making sure he didn't mess with the records without her knowledge. He'd have pondered it more if he hadn't been on the edge of his seat about Beaumont.

Since 5 a.m., every time his phone rang, he expected it to be the bad news that would destroy Colborn Aerospace forever. It was coming up on four as he paced his way through the great room toward the staircase, two thoughts on his mind. One, it was well past the end of business in France. And two, perhaps Darci was feeling ill.

He was about to check the guest room, when Justin burst in.

"Where's a television?" Justin barked.

"What? Why?"

"Closest television. Where is it?"

"Over there." Shane pointed to an alcove.

"Channel thirty-seven, Berkley Nash."

Shane could hardly believe it. "Not Bianca again."

"No, no. Not Bianca. Darci."

Shane was stunned. He could barely force out the words. "Darci's on Berkley Nash?"

She'd do that to him? She was *doing that* to him?

Justin scrambled for the remote control, tuning to the correct channel.

Shane would never forgive her for this. Absolutely never.

The picture came up on the screen. The flash title across the bottom read "Shane Colborn—Another Corporate Scandal?"

"I can't believe this." Shane dropped into an armchair, bracing himself.

There was Darci, looking poised and beautiful in a tailored black-and-white dress. Everything inside him knotted in anger.

"You were saying," said Berkley Nash, "that Dalton Colborn stole your father's invention."

"I was saying there is some disagreement between the two families about who was responsible for the original intellectual property."

Berkley frowned. "But you believe your father's turbine plans were stolen."

"My father indicated one of his inventions had been exploited by his former partner, Dalton Colborn."

"And Shane Colborn is stonewalling you."

Darci smiled and took a breath.

"Here it comes," said Justin.

"While Shane Colborn disagrees with my assessment of that particular situation," she said, "as I've gotten to know him, I've learned he's upstanding and professional."

"He disagrees with you?" Berkley prompted, obviously trying to zero in on the conflict.

"He does," said Darci. "And that makes it a testament to his honesty and principles that he's given me unfettered access to the company's records."

"What's she doing?" Shane said out loud.

"Would you say you've gotten to know him well?" asked Berkley.

"I think she's helping you," said Justin, clearly puzzled.

"Very well," said Darci.

"So, you have a *personal relationship* with Shane Colborn?" Berkley put a wealth of meaning into his tone and expression. "I expect that impacted his decision to give you unfettered access."

"Danger," said Justin.

Shane stilled.

"I'm not in a romantic relationship with Shane Colborn, if that's what you're asking."

"Come on, Ms. Rivers. Be honest with the viewers. From what we hear, Shane Colborn only has one kind of a relationship with beautiful women."

"Is this live?" asked Shane. Not that he could stop it. The whole thing would be over before he got anywhere near downtown Chicago.

"I'll be honest, Mr. Nash. I was spying on Shane for several weeks, undercover at Colborn Aerospace. When he discovered my dishonesty, instead of throwing me out on my ear, he offered to help me."

Shane looked to Justin. "What on earth?"

"So, you're not sleeping with Shane Colborn?"

"No, I am not."

"Not technically," Shane muttered under his breath. Not at the moment. Berkley hadn't asked her if she'd *ever* slept with Shane.

"Forgive me, Ms. Rivers," said Berkley, clearly frustrated with the direction of the interview. "But after all we've heard from people like Bianca Covington, it's hard to buy this white-knight story you're feeding us."

"I wouldn't describe Shane Colborn as a white knight."

"How would you—?"

"I would describe him as an ethical and professional businessman."

"And would—"

"Bianca Covington and any other jilted lovers can sling all the mud they want, but as a former Colborn Aerospace employee, and as a person in an adversarial relationship with Mr. Colborn, I have to be honest and say that I respect him as both a man and a CEO."

"You believe Bianca Covington was slinging mud?"

"I believe Bianca Covington was a woman scorned."

Berkley grinned, clearly delighted at the new swing in the conversation. "Bianca Covington may have something to say about that."

"I'm guessing she would. But I doubt she'll come after me."

"Why not?"

"Because my name on the cover of a scandalous book won't sell nearly as many copies."

"Here we go," Berkley sing-songed, practically rubbing his hands together with glee.

"We should be paying her," said Justin.

"Are you accusing Bianca Covington of libel?" Berkley asked.

"I'm saying Shane Colborn is too much of a gentleman to accuse her of lying."

"But you're saying she is."

"I'm saying the Shane Colborn I've come to know wouldn't have done any of the things in the book."

"What about the poetry?"

Darci's expression flinched ever so slightly, and Shane found himself tensing.

"That he recited in bed," Berkley prompted.

"To each his own," she said smoothly. "Personally, I'm fond of champagne, candlelight and long walks on the beach."

Berkley looked into the camera. "Take note of that, Chicago bachelors."

The music came up, and the camera panned away. Shane rocked back in his chair.

"I'm forwarding a link to Beaumont," said Justin, punching buttons on his phone.

"Why would she do it?" asked Shane, more to himself than to Justin.

"Because it wasn't fair." Darci's voice came from behind them.

Shane turned to find her standing at the edge of the alcove. He instantly rocked to his feet. She still wore the tailored dress, along with the sexiest black pumps he'd ever seen. Her hair was swooped up, her makeup perfect, and her face was framed with dangling crystal earrings and a matching necklace.

"Why did you do it?" he repeated.

"What she did to you wasn't fair."

"Lots of things aren't fair."

He struggled to see her angle. Did she think he could help her? Did she think he wasn't already helping her? Did she assume he was holding back and this would tip the balance in her favor?

Darci took a couple of steps forward. "I couldn't let eight hundred people lose their jobs."

"It wasn't your problem."

She shrugged her slender shoulders. "I don't know how—"

"Why are you grilling her?" Justin demanded. "She just saved us."

"It doesn't feel right," said Shane, approaching her at an angle, still working it through in his mind.

"What? You've got spidey senses now?" asked Justin.

"What would feel right?" Darci asked, stopping in front of him.

"The truth."

"Maybe I'm just an ethical person."

"Nah, that can't be it." But he couldn't help smiling.

"It's the best explanation you're going to get."

He found himself desperately wanting to believe her.

Justin brushed past them. "I'll try to set up a conference call with Beaumont. You okay to get up on European time tomorrow?" he called back to Shane.

"Whatever you need."

"I'll phone you later."

Shane was vaguely aware of Justin disappearing around the corner, but his gaze was tunneling to Darci.

"I owe you," he told her.

She gave a sad smile. "There's only one thing I want from you."

He knew that. "I wish there were two." The words were out before he had a chance to censor them.

She squeezed her eyes shut for a moment, but he moved forward, deciding to step right into the risk.

"Is there nothing else you want from me?" he asked in a low tone. "Nothing at all?"

"Shane."

"Tell me no." Then he was terrified she would. "Or tell me how bad it would be. On a scale of one to ten, how bad would it be for us to give in and make love again?"

She opened her eyes, those beautiful, crystal-green eyes that seemed to reach right down into his soul. In a blinding flash, he realized how desperately he'd missed her.

"Eight," she whispered.

Eight. That was a very high number. But he wasn't willing to give up. "Scale of one to ten, how bad do you want to do it anyway?"

She hesitated. "Ten."

"Eleven."

Humor warmed the color of her irises. "You just had to beat me there, didn't you?"

He reached out, gently taking her hand, twining his fingers around hers. "I'm definitely ahead of you on that score. Because if you wanted me as badly as I want you, we'd already be in my bed."

Her chest rose with an indrawn breath. "I've never seen your bed."

"It's a great bed. I bought the best."

"I bought a mismatched floor demo from Frugal One Warehouse."

"You should probably try mine."

"I might get spoiled."

"We can only hope." He took another half step, and his thighs brushed hers.

Her voice dropped to a whisper. "This is a really bad idea."

"This is a ridiculous idea." He cradled her face with his palms. "But for some reason I've stopped caring."

He leaned in slowly, forcing himself to take his time, giving her plenty of opportunity to bolt.

She didn't, and he kissed her.

He deepened the kiss, and as his hand sank into her hair, he reveled in its soft texture and the subtle scent of wildflowers.

She drew him closer. It felt so natural to be holding her. She belonged here in his embrace.

A voice sounded in the far reaches of the mansion, and he was reminded they weren't completely alone.

"Come on," he whispered against her lips, using his hand on the small of her back to urge her toward the staircase.

Wordlessly, she went with him, crossing the great room, then mounting the curved oak stairs.

Halfway up, she put a palm on the rail, slipping it along the polished surface. "We're really doing this."

He bent his head down to brush a kiss on her temple. "Yes. We are. It's right."

"I don't trust you."

"I know."

"I'm still out to get you."

"I know. But I also know you're scrupulously fair."

"Are you?" she asked.

"Yes," he said.

"So when we find the proof?"

"Darci?"

"Yes?"

They continued up the stairs until they reached a a landing. He gestured to an open pair of double doors. "This is my bedroom."

"Oh."

He placed his hands on her waist and guided her in. "Everything else can wait."

"Oh, Shane," she sighed. "This doesn't make sense."

"Life doesn't usually make sense."

On impulse, he lifted her into his arms, and she gasped in surprise before relaxing against his chest.

He kissed her mouth as he strode across the deep carpet. There was no need for a light. Twilight shone dimly through the paned windows, and he knew every inch of the room.

He set her down slowly, marveling that she was in his bedroom. He cradled her face, and she smiled up at him. Her cheeks were flushed, her lips slightly parted.

"You are astonishingly beautiful," he said.

She reached up to cover his hands "You are amazing. How do you do that?"

A fan whirled lazily above his authentic four-poster bed, which was piled with a steel-gray quilt and matching black throw pillows.

He kissed her with all the passion he was feeling, then he

circled his arms around her, lifting her from the floor. He wanted their kisses to go on and on.

He'd lain awake in this room countless times, wishing her here, willing her here. And now, she was. And she was his once again.

Her hands went to the buttons on his shirt, working her way down, her fingertips leaving a trail of heat on his skin. Her hands were so small, caresses so delicate. He reveled in her touch, closing his eyes to focus on the pads of her fingers, the graze of her nails.

Growing impatient, he found the zipper at the back of her dress, drawing it down, savoring the satin of her bare skin. He encountered the strap of her bra. He couldn't wait to see it, to remove it, to strip off the rest of her underwear and see her totally naked, feel her naked. His muscles hardened to iron in anticipation.

She tugged his shirt from the waistband of his pants, pushing it off his shoulders, letting it fall to the floor. Then she feathered her hands along his bare chest. Her expression was playful as she raised her arms. He tugged the dress up over her head, leaving it to one side.

He drew back, taking in her tanned shoulders, a lacy white bra, high-cut satin panties, and those delectable high heels.

"I can't believe you're finally here."

"Am I late?" she teased.

"Yes. Yes you are." It was the truth. "I've been waiting my entire life."

Her expression sobered. "Oh, Shane."

He slipped the strap of her bra down her arm.

"Darci." He kissed her bare shoulder.

He released the catch and left the bra with her dress. His hand enclosed one rounded breast, and he felt the tight nipple bead beneath his palm.

She groaned and leaned in. She kissed him hard, her tongue tangling with his, while her hands fumbled with the button on his pants.

Keen to help her, he kicked off his shoes, stepped out of his pants, and in seconds, they were naked, falling to the bed, his bed, fulfilling his wildest fantasies. But this was better than any of his fantasies. She was truly here.

He positioned himself on top, drinking in her beautiful face as he settled between her legs. Their lips met and he felt at once as if he'd found his home. Yet his heart was soaring, a sensation he'd never felt with any other woman.

Soon, kisses were not enough, and his hands roamed her body, reacquainting him with all of her secrets. She moaned at his touch, even as her hands began an exploration of their own. In minutes, need was throbbing through him.

He found a condom and then he reached beneath her, canting her hips upward.

"Yes," she whispered.

She grasped his shoulders tightly, her legs instantly wrapped around his waist. Her heat cradled his length, and the world seemed to achieve perfect harmony.

"I've missed you," he rasped. "I've missed you so much."

"I'm addicted," she said, before kissing him deeply.

His passion rose so quickly, it was almost frightening. He had to slow things down. He had to make this last.

He rolled to his back. But that was worse.

He sat up, her astride him. His gaze caught hers, her moss green eyes bright with need.

The world stopped, his motion, his breathing, his very heartbeat.

"Shane?" she asked in confusion.

He couldn't let her go. No matter what happened, he could never let her go. She belonged with him and nowhere else.

"You okay?" she asked.

"I'm perfect."

He moved again, and her eyes fluttered closed.

"That is so…"

She didn't need to finish the sentence. He cupped her breast again.

"Oh, yes," she said, matching his rhythm. Stronger and stronger she pressed. "Don't stop. Please, don't stop."

"I'm never stopping. Not ever, ever, *ever*."

She hugged him tight, as if she were holding on for all she was worth.

It felt good.

Everything felt good.

He knew he was losing the battle for control. And then she cried out, and he let go, and release cascaded through him.

Their hearts were thudding, their lungs dragging in oxygen. The room came back into focus around him, while her supple body turned limp in his arms.

"You okay?" he asked.

She gave a slow nod against his shoulder.

"You're incredible." He gathered her close.

Her voice was breathy. "That really was an eight."

He wasn't sure how to take that. "Only an eight?"

She must have heard the worry in his voice because she chuckled, her body vibrating against his. "The *idea* was an eight, an eight on the scale of smart to stupid."

"So, not the sex," he confirmed.

She lifted her head to look at him. "The sex was an eleven, Shane."

"Twelve."

She rolled her eyes. "You just *had* to beat me."

He pushed back a wisp of her hair. "You beat me." He kissed her. "You blew me away. I don't even know what to do about this."

Darci awoke in Shane's bed, her back curled against him, his arm draped across her stomach. His breathing was deep and easy. From the light beyond the windows, she guessed it was about six.

She hadn't paid much attention last night, but the bedroom was enormous. The king-size bed was directly across from a white stone fireplace. The details and furnishings were ornate, the style masculine. At one end of the rectangular room, a bank of bay windows and a set of French doors overlooked the grounds. The doors opened onto a small balcony.

Shane's arm tightened around her, and he kissed her shoulder.

"Morning," he said in a sleepy voice.

"Morning." She shifted around to face him and met his gaze. "Nice bed you've got here."

"Are you spoiled yet?"

"I am."

"Good. Stay."

She couldn't help but smile. "Sure. Why not?" She waited a beat. "Wait a minute. There's a long list of reasons why not."

"I'm going to help you," he said.

"Write the list?"

"Look for the drawings."

"I thought you were already—" She sat up, twisting to face him. "Have you been holding out on me? Do you know something—?"

"I haven't been holding out on you." He sat up beside her. "Calm down, Darci. I still think you're wrong."

She frowned.

"But I'll leave no stone unturned. I'll show you anything you want to see, take you anywhere you want to go. And when we don't find your proof, you'll have to believe me."

"You look like you're expecting me to say thank you."

"I'm not. That's not what this is about. This is about finding the truth."

"I already know the truth."

He looped his arm around her waist and pushed her back onto the bed, looming over her. "You are the most stubborn woman I have ever met."

"And you are the most hardheaded man in the world."

But she liked being in his arms. She felt good in his arms. And when he leaned in to kiss her, she kissed him back. It took only seconds for the kiss to grow passionate.

Unexpectedly, he stopped. "We have work to do."

"Huh?"

"I have to call Justin about the French, and you have more file boxes to search."

"Oh, yeah. I know that. I just thought..."

A self-satisfied smile grew on his face. "We'll get to that, too. Later."

"Later?"

"I assumed you'd want to sleep in this decadent bed again tonight."

It felt as if she ought to object to his assumption. Then again, only seconds ago, she'd leapt to her own conclusion that they would make love again. It was hard to know which of them was more presumptuous. It was likely a wash.

"Sure," she agreed. "I probably won't be through searching."

"I hope I don't have to go to France."

"You think you might?" She'd be disappointed, but she'd learned a lot about Colborn Aerospace over the past few days, and she understood how important the contract was to the company.

"Let's find out." He sat up and reached for his phone, tapped the screen and put it to his ear.

"You should come with me," he said as the call rang through.

It was tempting. "I'm not going to France."

"Why not?"

"I have work to do."

"It's not like you have a job. I was there when you got fired, remember?"

She hit him with his pillow. "I quit."

"You lied to the boss."

"The boss is a fraud."

Shane spoke into the phone. "Hey, Justin."

He paused, his gaze sliding to Darci. "I am cheerful."

She felt her cheeks heat. It wasn't going to take much for Justin to put two and two together.

"They did?" Shane's voice was serious again.

Darci held her breath. No matter what happened between her and Shane, she didn't want to see any jobs lost. She'd met quite a few Colborn employees while she was there. They were great people, and they didn't deserve to get caught in the middle.

"That's a surprise," said Shane. He reached out and squeezed Darci's hand.

"Later," he said to Justin, signing off.

"They didn't cancel?" Darci guessed.

Shane shook his head. "They're signing."

Her chest tightened. "For sure?"

"For sure."

"But you're still retooling for the private-jet market? Because diversification is never a bad idea."

"You do know you're off the payroll, right?"

She gave a self-conscious smile. "I still have ears."

"You're also naked. I'm getting business advice from a naked goddess."

"You're not a sexist, are you?"

"Not at all. I'm just wondering where my life went wrong that *this* conversation we're having in my bed. Am I getting old and staid?"

"You want to go back to eighteenth-century poetry?"

His expression faltered, and for a second, she thought she'd gone too far.

"You're definitely not Bianca," he said softly.

"I'm assuming that's a good thing."

He set the phone aside and slipped his arm beneath her waist again, leaning her back, a calculating expression on his face. "Everything about you is good, Darci Rivers."

"I thought we were getting back to work?"

"Later." He kissed her long and hard. "Much later."

Eleven

Shane was oddly disheartened at having to admit defeat, or victory, he supposed, depending on how you looked at it.

In the wine cellar late Saturday afternoon, Darci closed the last of the file boxes, rubbing her palms across the smooth, cardboard top.

"Nothing," she said out loud.

Jennifer, who had spent the day helping, reached out to squeeze her shoulder. "I'm so sorry."

"I'm sorry, too," said Shane, fighting the urge to draw Darci into his arms.

She shot him an impatient look. "No, you're not."

"I am." He couldn't honestly say he was surprised. And he'd admit it was the best outcome for both him and Colborn Aerospace. But he was sorry she was disappointed after all her hard work.

"You're allowed to gloat now," she told him.

"I don't want to gloat."

"It was a long shot," Jennifer said to Darci, giving her another squeeze.

Justin appeared in the doorway, a tablet computer in his hand. "Signed, sealed and delivered."

He glanced up and took in everyone's expressions. "What happened?"

"That was the last box," said Shane, nodding to where Darci was sitting at the big table.

"So, no surprises?" asked Justin.

"No surprises," remarked Darci.

"Makes my life easier," said Justin.

"Don't be a jerk," said Shane.

"What?" Justin looked genuinely perplexed. "Did any of you really think it was going to go the other way?"

"I did," said Jennifer.

"You obviously never met Ian Rivers."

"Don't insult my father," said Darci.

"Justin," Shane cautioned.

"What? Are you running a business or an emotional-support group?"

"You don't have to behave like a classless jerk."

"At least he's honest," said Darci.

"*I'm* being honest," said Shane.

"So, are we relocating back to the office?" asked Justin, sounding eager.

"Not yet," said Shane. He didn't know what he wanted to do next, but leaving Darci wasn't it.

"We don't know anything for sure," said Darci.

She came to her feet, lifting the box.

Shane quickly moved to take it from her and put it on the trolley.

"Just because there's no proof," she continued. "Doesn't mean it never happened."

"You're grasping at straws," said Justin. "But you're right. I can't prove a negative."

"We're all tired," said Shane. "And we're all hungry."

"I'm not tired," said Justin. He glanced at his watch.

Shane ignored him. "Let's go get some fresh air. I'll fire up the barbecue. Jennifer, grab us some wine."

Jennifer's eyes rounded, and she glanced around the cellar. "You want me to pick something out?"

"Go for it," he said.

"I don't have a clue what I'm doing." But she was grinning from ear to ear as she looked around.

"It's hard to go wrong in here."

"You think you can appease us with good wine?" asked Darci.

"I think I can get you drunk on good wine."

"Take something from the top shelf," Darci said to Jennifer.

Shane chuckled. "In that case, I'll see if the cook has any filets."

"You've got something against burgers and Bordeaux?" asked Darci.

"You became an expert fast."

"I'm…" Her expression sobered. "I'm really not in the mood to joke around."

This time, he did move to her, drawing her into his arms. "I know you're disappointed."

Out of the corner of his eye, he saw Justin and Jennifer exchange a look. He didn't know how much they'd guessed. And he didn't know how much Darci had shared. But she'd spent the past two nights in his bed, and he wasn't about to pretend there was nothing between them.

"I'm not giving up," she said against his chest.

"Okay." He wasn't exactly sure what more she could do.

What were the options? What would he do if it was him?

He would see it through. And so would she. She tipped her chin up. "You won't get in my way?"

"I said I'd help, didn't I?" He was positive there was nothing to find. But he was going to support her for as long as it took for her to accept reality.

He gave her a squeeze, thinking how much he'd like to kiss her.

"You guys want us to leave you alone?" asked Jennifer.

"Yes," said Shane.

Just as Darci said, "No."

Darci playfully smacked her palm into the center of his chest and moved away. "Top shelf, Jen. It's the very least he owes us."

Shane gave in and headed for the door. "I'll go see about some steaks."

Justin fell into step beside him as they headed down the hall.

"What was that?" asked Justin.

"What?"

"You, Darci. Hey, I know she's hot—"

"She's more than hot."

"What exactly is going on between you two?"

"None of your business."

"I'm your lawyer. Everything's my business."

"Not my sex life."

"Your sex life is what causes me most of my headaches."

"Darci's not going to cause you any headaches."

"Are you hearing yourself?"

They reached the staircase and turned to go up.

"She won't," Shane tossed over his shoulder.

"She threatened to write another tell-all book."

"It was an idle threat."

"You can't know that."

At the top of the stairs, Shane turned toward the kitchen. "She truly believes she's right."

"No kidding. That's what makes her dangerous."

Shane slowed his steps, realizing he had to come at this from a different angle. Up to now, he'd been reactive, letting Darci take the lead. The question wasn't what he'd do if he was her. The question was what he could do to find the answer.

"Could you find something to prove she's wrong?" he asked Justin.

"You mean prove that Dalton created the schematics?"

"Yes. It's not enough that she can't verify she's right."

"Legally speaking, yes it is."

"I'm not speaking legally. I need to be able to prove she's wrong."

They neared the kitchen door.

"So you can keep sleeping with her?"

Shane stopped. "Watch it, Justin."

"I need all the facts, Shane. I can't give you proper legal advice without them."

"It's not just sex," said Shane.

"Then I need to know that, too. If your judgment is clouded, if you're not operating in the best interest of Colborn Aerospace—"

"I *own* Colborn Aerospace."

"And I have a responsibility to *you*."

"My judgment isn't clouded."

Justin frowned. "Can we at least be honest?"

Shane drew a breath and opened his mouth to defend his

position. Then he thought better of it. What was the truth? Could he honestly say Darci wasn't clouding his judgment?

If he didn't like her, if he wasn't sleeping with her, if instead she'd been some graying old man coming forward with the same claim, what would he do?

"You're right," he said.

"I'm always right," said Justin.

"My judgment is ridiculously clouded. I can't even see straight where it comes to Darci."

"That's why you need me."

"Okay." Shane gave a decisive nod. "I'll take your advice. So, tell me honestly, is there any downside to finding concrete proof of my father's innocence? Is that a completely irrational thing to do?"

"It only uses up my time."

"Staff it out. Put someone else on it."

Justin paused for a beat. "That I can do."

"Good."

Proof positive was what Shane needed. Once Darci understood that his father hadn't swindled hers, they could focus on themselves. They could see where this relationship was going. His judgment might be clouded, but he knew she was special. And he wasn't about to mess this up.

"This is off the charts," said Jennifer, twirling in a circle on the mansion's lawn.

They'd set the wine bottles on a table at the pool deck and were admiring the view across the rose garden.

"Everything about Shane Colborn is off the charts," said Darci.

She wished she could dislike him. But whenever she let her guard down, she seemed to default to liking him.

"So, what are you going to do now?" Jennifer asked in a softer voice.

"I'm going to keep looking."

Her father had been too distraught for too many years for there to be nothing to the story. Maybe the truth wasn't exactly what she'd guessed, but there had to be some kind of foundation to his claim.

"Is there anywhere left to look?"

"I don't know," Darci confessed.

There hadn't been any promising leads at the corporate headquarters, and Shane had told her none of the D&I Holdings records had been copied or scanned into the computer system. He also said Dalton hadn't kept any private files at the office. Shane had been using Dalton's former office at Colborn Aerospace for years now. If there'd been anything stashed away there, he'd have long since come across it.

Strangely, she believed him. Which meant she must trust him on some level.

"And Shane?" asked Jennifer. "What are you going to do about him?"

"I don't know about that, either."

"He likes you," said Jennifer.

"He likes sleeping with me."

"And you like sleeping with him."

Darci caught sight of Shane and Justin following the concrete path from the mansion. They were a hundred yards away and still out of earshot. Shane's stride was long and easy, his shoulders powerful over an extraordinarily fit body. He looked at home here, like a man at one with and in charge of his surroundings.

"What's not to like?" she asked.

Jennifer followed the line of her sight. "Have you got it bad?"

"I don't know what I've got. He's not what I expected."

"Do you think he's being straight with you about the drawings?"

The two men grew closer.

"Are you asking if I think he destroyed the original drawings?"

"Or he knows that his father destroyed them."

Darci had thought about that. "It's impossible to know for sure. I might never know for sure."

Shane reached the edge of the pool deck and stopped to examine the two bottles of wine.

"Now, this is disappointing," he called out. His gaze zeroed in on Jennifer. "These aren't from the top shelf."

"You can't have that place memorized," Jennifer responded.

Shane handed the bottles to Justin. "Take her back inside and let her have another go."

"They were near the top," said Darci, moving toward the pool deck.

"The labels are pretty," said Jennifer.

Shane rolled his eyes.

"Let's go," said Justin, cocking his head at the house.

"It was Darci who stopped me," said Jennifer, coming to a halt in front of Justin.

"Oh, sure. Blame me."

Justin's eyes twinkled. "I'll steer you in the right direction."

"Better hurry," said Shane. "A steward's coming down with cocktails."

Justin motioned for Jennifer to go first, and they started up the path.

Shane grasped Darci's hand, tugging her with him.

She nearly stumbled. "What?"

"We've got about ten minutes."

"Ten minutes to what?"

He pulled her behind the screen of the pool house, spinning her around so that her back was to the sun-warmed wall.

"This." He leaned down and kissed her. "I've been dying to do that all day."

"You're nuts."

"I'm nuts about you." He kissed her again, lingering this time, delving deeper, easing his body full-length against hers.

It felt wonderful, and she gave into the sensation.

He drew back, but only inches, resting his forehead against hers. "Stay," he said. "Stay tonight. I know the search is over, but I don't want you to leave."

It was tempting. It was incredibly tempting to set reality aside and simply stay here in his arms.

"What are we doing, Shane?"

"Enjoying each other's company."

"This isn't what I wanted. This isn't what I planned."

"I know." He gave her another soft, brief kiss. "It's blind-sided me, too."

"As a friend once told me, this isn't going to end well," she persevered.

"We'll handle it."

"Will you? Will you really?"

He kissed her again. "Yes, I will."

"And when I'm right?"

"So far, you're not."

"But if I am?"

"And I have to give you half a billion dollars?"

The statement startled her. "Is *that* what you think I'm after?"

He smiled, his hands settling around her rib cage. "What else would you be after?"

She could barely believe it. "Are you joking? You think I want *half* of Colborn Aerospace?"

"Darci, you've just spent weeks—"

"I want fair-market value for my Dad's intellectual property. At the time he left the company. Plus interest, sure, because that would be reasonable. But mostly, I want you and everyone else to acknowledge his contribution to the industry. He created a revolutionary, award-winning jet-engine innovation, and nobody knows about it."

"You're not out to get control of Colborn?"

"You thought I wanted control of Colborn?"

He searched her expression. "Yes. Sure. Of course."

"Because that's what you would do?" she asked.

"That's what anyone would do."

"I'm not anyone."

His expression smoothed out. "No, you're not." He kissed her again.

"Stop," she sputtered.

"No."

"We're *fighting*."

"We've stopped. Now we're kissing."

"Shane."

But his next kiss muffled her protest. Her body responded to him. Her lips softened, and her eyes fluttered closed.

"You're cheating," she sighed.

"You're spying," he responded.

"Not anymore."

"Only because I caught you." He kissed her again, bringing a telling moan from the depths of her chest.

"Stay," he repeated, his voice low and commanding.

It was what she wanted. She couldn't deny it.

She gave in. "Just one more night."

"One more night," he echoed, his hands tightening beneath her breasts, his expression turning possessive.

Shane watched Darci pad barefoot across his bedroom. First, studying the photos on his shelves, then peering out the bay window into the darkness before running her fingertips across the top of his dresser. She'd slipped his discarded shirt over her shoulders, and it fell to midthigh of her shapely legs. Lying in his messy bed, he could still feel the imprint where those thighs had been wrapped around his waist. He decided there was no better view than a tousled-haired, half-dressed Darci wandering around his bedroom.

"Was this your parents' room?" she asked, moving toward the walk-in closet.

"No," he answered. "Theirs was at the front of the house."

"You didn't move in to the master bedroom after they died?"

Shane shrugged. "I like this room."

"You didn't want to be lord of the manor?"

He gave a low chuckle. "I'd hardly call this a manor."

"I would."

"There are plenty of houses bigger than this."

She tested the knob and opened the closet door a couple of inches. "How many bedrooms?"

"Seven."

"Staff quarters?"

"Above the garage and beside the pool house."

She sent him a questioning look and gestured to the closet door. "Do you mind?"

"Knock yourself out."

As far as he could remember, there weren't any embarrassing secrets in his closet. And, if there were, the housekeeping staff would have discovered them years ago.

She pulled open the door.

"Light switch on the right," he told her.

"You're very cooperative."

"I do try."

She flipped on the switch. "What's in here?"

"Suits mostly, shoes, ties. There might be an old briefcase and a couple of watches lying around. Oh, and if you open the secret panel behind the third shelf, you'll find the original turbine plans that prove your father's story."

"Ha, ha." She disappeared inside.

"Is that what you're looking for?" he called.

"I don't know what I'm looking for." There was a silence. "Hang on."

He waited for her to elaborate.

"Now *that's* not something you see every day."

"What?"

"Oh, Shane. You should have said something."

"Huh?" He tossed back the covers and climbed out of bed.

She giggled from inside the closet.

He paced across the floor, coming to the entrance of the closet and grasping both sides of the jamb. "What are you—"

She stood in the middle of his closet, a saucy grin on her face, a pair of tiger-striped boxer shorts held up to her waist.

"They're you," she sing-songed.

"They were a gift."

"Uh-huh. Sure they were."

"The tags are still attached."

She held them out. "Put 'em on."

"Not a chance."

She pouted. "I bet they're sexy."

"Then you put them on."

"Yeah?" She waggled her brows.

"I dare you," he said.

"You *dare* me?"

"I do."

She lowered them to her knees, bending over, lifting one foot to step in. The dress shirt gaped open, only two buttons fastening it, giving him an excellent view.

"Take your time," he told her.

She looked up and stuck out her tongue, turning him on even more. Then she pulled them up to her waist, fisting the fabric at the back so they wouldn't fall down.

"What do you think?"

He stepped forward, grinning. "Oh, baby."

She did a pirouette. "We don't need fancy lingerie."

"You wear lingerie?"

"What woman doesn't?"

"Where is it? Can you get it? Let's go."

She laughed.

He wrapped an arm around her waist, settling her close. "You look ridiculous."

"Not as ridiculous as you'd have looked."

"You took a bullet for me," he crooned.

"That's the kind of woman I am."

For some reason, the teasing went out of him, and he sobered. "I like the kind of woman you are."

Her smile disappeared. "Shane, don't."

"Don't what?"

"Don't be serious. I can't do this if you're going to be serious."

"I seriously want you." He flicked open the two buttons on the shirt, splaying his hand inside, moving across her rib cage around to the smooth skin of her back.

"I look ridiculous," she whispered.

"You look beautiful. You always look beautiful. I can't imagine anyone more beautiful than you."

He leaned down to leave a path of kisses along her shoulder. Her skin was warm, smooth, fragrant.

She murmured, "I'm still working against you."

"I know." But he truly didn't care.

"I'm in here, searching for evidence."

"I know that, too."

He couldn't resist, so he closed one hand over her breast. As he caressed her, her nipple beaded against his palm, hijacking his senses.

He reached for her hand, releasing the fingers that gripped the tiger-print fabric. She let the silly shorts drop to the floor. The shirt gaped open, and her skin was hot against his.

"My plan," she told him breathlessly.

He began to lower to the carpet, bringing her with him.

"My plan," she repeated, even as she went willingly with him.

He sat on the floor then and she slipped sweetly onto his lap. She ran her fingers through his hair.

"I like you like this," he breathed.

She drew in a couple of deep breaths. "My plan was to wait until you were asleep and ransack your father's room."

"I'll help you," said Shane.

"You shouldn't help me."

He anchored her hips. "I can't get enough of you."

Her head dropped back and she moaned as she brought them together as one.

He kissed her jawline, her cheek and then her mouth. He drank in every intoxicating move of her hips. She was hot and slick, and her scent clung to him.

Though they'd just made love, he felt as if this was their first time. His passion held no patience. He went from zero to a thousand in a single breath. He was terrified he'd leave her behind, he wanted to slow things down, but his primal nature had taken over.

"Shane," she purred in his ear. "Oh, Shane." Her voice was silky smooth as she spurred him on, repeating his name over and over.

And then her purring turned to loud gasps and she cried out in pleasure. He followed her, doing the same, relishing sensation after sensation. What if he'd never found this woman?

He held her tight, sweat gathered between them. Their

hearts were pounding in time to one another's as they both struggled for air.

"That was…" He started the sentence but couldn't find the right adjective. Nothing was strong enough. Nothing was good enough.

"Distracting," she said.

He managed a smile. "That wasn't where I was going."

"We're in your closet."

"I noticed."

"I've never had sex in a closet."

"I've never had sex with someone in tiger-print shorts."

She chuckled, her body still resting against his.

"To think I once hated those shorts."

"Do you still hate them?" she asked.

"I think I love them." His arms tightened around her.

She chuckled. Then she drew a deep breath. "I meant what I said."

"What did you say?" He cast his mind back, hoping it was something great. Like she wanted to stay with him, live with him forever, maybe have his children.

"As soon as you're asleep, I'm ransacking your father's old room."

"What are you hoping to find?"

"I don't know. A signed confession, maybe."

"I'll give you a hand."

"You've got bad karma. You're hoping I'll fail."

"The confession is either there, or it isn't. Karma's not going to make it appear."

"You mean disappear."

"You're grasping at straws again, Darci."

"I don't care."

He cradled her cheeks, putting just enough space between their faces so he could focus. "Are you ever going to say die?"

"Not yet."

"Can you live with it if you're wrong? Can you live with me if you're wrong?"

"Can you live with it if I'm right?"

"Yes." It was such a far-fetched idea that Shane didn't even have to think about it.

"Then let's go look."

She buttoned the shirt back up and rose from his lap.

Then, with a mischievous grin, she tossed him the garish shorts.

He gave a shrug, pulled them on.

"I officially love these shorts," he said as he got to his feet.

He took her hand and led her to the bedroom door, out into the hallway, and down three doors to the master.

It had been months, maybe years since he'd been inside. It wasn't kept as a shrine or anything. In fact, guests had stayed here many times. But it wasn't Shane's room, and it never would be.

He turned on the light, and Darci gasped, latching on to his arm.

"Why didn't you tell me?" she demanded.

"Tell you what?"

His gaze darted around the room. He was confused. Nothing looked out of place.

"This." She made a beeline across the floor.

"What?"

"This," she repeated, spreading her hands across the walnut desk sitting against the far wall.

"It's not a secret desk."

"It's old."

He followed her across the room. "My dad had it for years."

She opened the top drawer. "It might have old things in it."

"It's empty, Darci."

She opened the right-hand drawer.

"It's empty," he repeated.

She opened the next drawer, moving faster, finding only a pen and a few stray paperclips.

"I'm sorry," he said, placing a hand gently on her shoulder.

She opened the last drawer to find it empty. Then she slammed it shut and turned into his arms.

Twelve

Though the desk had been unfortunately empty, it had inspired Darci to look further. There could have been other things she'd missed in this big place. There was nothing to say the records room was the only cache of company information.

After breakfast, she told Shane she was checking the other rooms in the mansion. With a fatalistic shake of his head, he waved her on her way, wishing her good luck. She didn't care that he was skeptical. She wasn't going to let it bother her.

She scoured the main floor but found nothing promising. The second floor was the same. By the end of the third floor, her confidence was flagging.

All that was left was the basement, and she'd been over most of it already.

In the basement hallway, she could hear Shane, Justin and a couple of other male voices in the distance. Justin was saying they had to pack up the wine cellar, get back to the office, and Shane was agreeing.

Darci didn't blame them. She knew deep down this was her last chance. She took the little passage that led to the records room, deciding to double check every shelf. Maybe something had been misfiled. Perhaps there were D&I Holdings boxes mixed in with the Colborn ones.

She started in the corner where the D&I Holdings boxes had been restacked. They were back in order, looking neat and tidy. The shelves cleaned beneath them. She ran her fingers across the smooth surface.

The cartons on the next shelf were from Colborn, from the earliest years of the company. They were dusty and aged, some of them askew. It was obvious nobody had opened them for years. She could only imagine they were as jumbled inside as the D&I Holdings records.

She straightened one, lining it up with the next. Then she straightened the container below that.

A label caught her eye, far down on the bottom shelf. It said "Colborn Aerospace, Patent Applications."

She bent her knees, crouching down, rereading the tag. Then she slid the box from its spot.

She took a deep breath, refusing to get her hopes up. She'd let herself get so excited so many times these past weeks— only to have her optimism ripped out from under her—and she refused to do it again.

She carefully peeled off the packing tape and bent open the lid.

She began to sort methodically through the documents. She found letters, instructions, forms, applications and registrations but nothing that mentioned a turbine.

Then, about halfway through the box, she came to a thick sheaf of papers. They were folded in four, a note clipped to the outside.

It was handwritten, and she recognized Dalton's handwriting. *Go ahead and file*, it said. *If he hasn't done it by now, he doesn't have them*.

Darci plunked her butt down on the concrete floor.

She slowly unfolded the pages. Then she blinked to refocus, barely believing what she saw.

They were photocopies of schematic drawings. They were labeled "turbine engine." There was no signature on the pages, but there was a suspicious bright white patch in the bottom corner. And Dalton's note was damning. *File* had to mean filing the patents. And the *he* had to refer to her father. This was Dalton telling somebody to file for the patents because he didn't think Ian had the original drawings.

Her body went cold with shock, then it turned hot with excitement. It was all true. Everything was true. And this was the proof.

She could barely catch her breath as she rose to her feet, steadying herself with one hand on the nearest shelf. She left the room in a daze, stumbling along the hallway toward the wine cellar. Shane's and the other voices grew louder as she drew near.

She rounded the corner to stand in the doorway. Her throat was dry, and she had to swallow a couple of times.

"I found it." The words came out as a whisper.

The four men stopped talking and stared at her, Shane, Justin, Tuck and another she didn't recognize. A minute ticked by.

"The drawings?" asked Shane.

She gave a nod, moving into the cellar. "It's a copy. But there's a note. It was written by Dalton."

"He signed it?" asked Justin, whisking the papers from her hands.

"No, but I recognize his handwriting. I've been reading things he wrote for days now." The D&I Holdings boxes had been full of notes and memos written by both her father and by Dalton.

"This could mean anything," said Justin, flipping through the pages.

"The note was clipped to a copy of the schematic drawings," said Darci. "They were in a box labeled 'Patent Applications.'"

Justin took two steps to the big table. He handed Shane the note and spread out the drawings.

"He's saying they should file the patent," Darci said to Shane. "*Him* means my father. And *them* are the original drawings. There's no other way to interpret it."

"There are about a hundred other ways to interpret it," said Justin, staring at the drawings.

The other two men moved in for a look.

"This is Dixon," Tuck said to Darci. "My brother."

Darci gave the man an absent nod.

"Hi, Darci," said Dixon.

Justin spoke to Darci. "There's nothing here that links the drawings to your father."

"They whited out his signature," said Darci, pointing to the curiously blank spot in the bottom corner.

She might not be much of a spy, but even she could figure out that much. "They whited out his signature, filed the patent with a photocopy of the drawings and counted on the originals never coming to light. What else can *he doesn't have them* mean?"

"That note doesn't contain a single proper noun," said Justin. "It could be about the bathroom sink, for all we know."

Darci glanced at Shane, trying to gauge his reaction. He looked shell-shocked.

"It was attached to schematic drawings of a turbine engine, not a bathroom sink," she told them both.

"So you say," said Justin.

"You think I'm lying?"

She looked to Shane for support. After all this time, he should know she wouldn't lie.

Before Shane could speak, Justin jumped in. "This isn't proof. We're not handing over half a billion dollars on some vague, handwritten note."

"I don't *want* half a billion dollars." insisted Darci. How many times did she have to say it?

"Yeah, right," said Justin.

She felt Tuck and Dixon's speculative gazes on her.

"Ask Shane." She glanced at him again. Why wouldn't he speak up? "I asked him for fair-market value at 1989 prices."

"That's it?" Tuck asked Darci, surprise in his tone.

She nodded to him. "Plus interest. Plus credit to my dad for the invention."

"Plus, plus, plus..." said Justin with conviction.

"It's perfectly fair," said Darci.

"And what will you want after that?" he asked.

Darci glared at him.

"Half of Colborn," said Dixon, his gaze calculating as he watched her.

"That's exactly what she wants," said Justin.

"I don't think she's like that," said Tuck.

"Hello?" said Darci. "You can see me standing here, right?"

"They're all like that," said Dixon.

"You're jaded," said Tuck.

"I'm realistic."

"What's the matter with you people?" Darci couldn't control her frustration any longer. Her attention went to Shane. "When you look at where I found it, what it says and what else we know, it proves Dalton stole the drawings."

"Not without signed originals," said Tuck. His gaze was a lot more sympathetic than anyone else's. "I'm sorry, Darci, but this doesn't do it."

She glared at the lot of them, ending with Shane.

When he finally spoke, his tone seemed sympathetic, and she experienced a glimmer of hope.

But then he spoke. "It's not that cut-and-dried."

He couldn't see it. Or he wouldn't see it. And she realized it hadn't been sympathy in his voice. It was caution.

And then it all made sense. She would have laughed if it wasn't so painful. She was naive, a babe in the woods. These men were closing ranks to protect their own interests.

"You were never going to believe," she said to Shane. "It didn't matter what I found, you'd have found a means to discredit it."

"You still need what you were looking for," said Shane. "You need the signed originals."

"Before you'll believe me?"

"There's too much at stake for—"

"No, Shane. There was never anything at stake for you. Because you were never going to let this happen. You've been stringing me along the whole time."

"No," he denied. "If you'd found the originals—"

"You'd have discredited them, too." Her chest tightened until it burned.

She wanted to scream, and she wanted to cry. But she knew neither of those things would help. She was a fool, and she'd been had.

With a shake of her head, she left them. Her heart turned to stone as she stormed along the basement hallway. She jogged up the staircase then trotted through the corridor and the great room before running down the front steps to where her car was parked in the drive.

She jumped inside, peeled away from the curb and sped out onto the main road, quickly bringing up her speed.

She'd been so certain Shane would accept the evidence. She'd thought he was on her side. She'd thought they had something special. She'd thought...

The truth leapt into her brain.

Her heart stuttered.

She hastily wheeled into a street-side parking lot and braked under a maple tree.

She dropped her head onto the steering wheel.

She'd thought she loved him.

She'd actually let herself believe the relationship was real. But Shane had a whole other agenda. Without absolute proof and a court of law, she was never going to win.

Her cell phone rang. She let it go to voice mail, her hands tightening on the steering wheel until her knuckles went white.

Long minutes later, she lifted her head, staring straight ahead at the riverbank in front of her.

Was it time to give up? Did she pack up her broken heart and go home? There was no way she could face Shane again, no way he'd let her look any further.

She opened her purse, extracting the letter from her father, unfolding it one more time. The words were so angry, so desperate. The hurt of the betrayal came through loud and clear in his writing.

Then her gaze went to the picture of him in the D&I Holdings office. He'd looked happy back then, hopeful and full of life. She wished she'd known that side of him.

"I tried," she whispered, hoping he'd have understood.

She stared at his face for a long time.

Then something else came into focus. The desk behind him. In fact, there were two desks behind him, facing each other, like hers and Jennifer's did. And they were identical.

Darci's heart began beating faster.

They were also the same as the one in Dalton's old bedroom. One of these desks was in Dalton's bedroom.

This had to be a clue. That was why the picture was with the letter. It showed the hiding place of the drawings.

She'd already checked one desk. But what about the other? Where was the other desk?

And then it hit her.

The other desk would have gone to her father. And if his desk held the drawings, he'd have had them all along. He wouldn't have needed anything from Dalton. He'd have simply presented the original drawings to a lawyer and won the case.

Unless the desks had been switched.

That was it. That had to be it. Her father had no way of getting into Dalton's mansion. If the furniture had been accidentally switched, he wouldn't have been able to retrieve the drawings.

She glanced at the road leading from the mansion to the city. As soon as Shane cleared out, she'd try one more time. She had to search the desk again.

Shane stared at his father's note, grappling between what was legal and what was moral.

"Don't go there," Justin warned him, obviously guessing at his thoughts.

"She's not wrong," said Shane.

"You can't trust her," said Dixon.

Shane looked up. "That's the problem. I do trust her."

"She threatened to write a tell-all book," said Justin, his voice rising.

"She could be just like Bianca," said Tuck.

"She's not like Bianca."

"She's like Kassandra," said Dixon.

Everybody went quiet.

"I trusted Kassandra," said Dixon. "And I fought with my father over her. I fought just as hard then as you're fighting now."

"It's not the same," said Shane.

"It's exactly the same. You think you can't live without her, but one day, she'll meet some slimy pharmaceutical ex-

ecutive, and a team of lawyers will try to take you for everything you've got."

"Divorce not going well?" Shane asked Dixon.

"It's going great. Because I was smart. Don't you be an
idiot."

"I'm not marrying her," said Shane. Though, as the words
came out, a vision of Darci in a long white dress came up in
his mind. She looked really good.

"She lied to you and spied on you," said Justin. "And that's
just the stuff we know about."

"I'm not giving her up," said Shane.

"At least wait."

"If I wait, I lose her."

"This is an unacceptable risk," said Justin, his posture rigid.

"It's mine to take."

"You take my advice on this. You take my advice on this,
or I'll walk."

Shane took in the conviction on his lawyer and best friend's
face. Justin was smart. He was brilliant. But he didn't know
Darci the way Shane did.

"Then walk," Shane said softly.

Justin threw up his hands in disgust.

"Wow," Tuck whistled.

"My father could easily have done it," Shane said to all of
them. "Legally provable or not, Dalton may have screwed Ian
Rivers over and stolen his money. And none of this is Darci's
fault. She's a fantastic person, and she's just trying to make
things right."

"Been there," said Dixon. "Done that."

"Could anybody have stopped you?" Shane asked.

Dixon didn't answer.

Justin groaned in obvious despair, bracing his hands on
the tabletop.

"Walk if you have to," Shane said to him. "But I'm going
after her."

"You are an idiot," said Justin.

"He's in love," said Dixon.

Shane didn't know about love. But he did know he wasn't giving up on Darci. He knew where she lived now, and that was where he was going.

He drove there as fast as he dared and parked in front of Darci's building and took the elevator. There were only two suites on the top floor, and he easily located hers. He was surprised to find the door slightly ajar.

"Because I *can't* just walk away from this," came a man's voice from inside the apartment.

There was a muffled exclamation from a woman

Shane broke into a run. He flung open the door to see a man's broad back. He was bent over a woman, obviously kissing her. She was standing passive, her arms by her sides.

Shane's momentum took him across the room, and he grabbed the guy by the back of the collar.

"Get your hands off her," he bellowed, spinning the stranger around and slamming him into the wall.

"Shane!"

He drew back his fist.

"Shane, don't!"

He suddenly realized it was Jennifer's voice, not Darci's.

The haze cleared from his brain.

Though the stranger was tall and obviously fit, the man simply held up his palms in surrender.

Shane stepped back, his attention going to Jennifer. "I thought you were Darci."

"Darci's at the mansion." Jennifer looked dazed.

"You okay?" Shane asked her, glancing at the stranger again.

"I'm fine. This is Ashton Watson."

"Your boyfriend?"

"Ex."

Shane crossed his arms over his chest. "Does he need to leave?"

"It looks like he does," said Ashton, with a reproachful gaze at Jennifer, "unless there's something more you want to say?"

She stayed silent, her lips compressed.

"I won't be back," said Ashton.

He gave Shane a curt nod and left the apartment, the door clicking shut behind him.

"I didn't mean to barge in," said Shane.

"It didn't change anything." Jennifer's voice shook ever so slightly. "What's going on? Where's Darci?"

"I'm looking for her."

"I thought she was at the mansion."

"She was. But she left." He hesitated, but given what he'd just witnessed, he decided Jennifer was entitled to the truth. "We had a fight."

She waited.

"Darci found something," said Shane.

"The drawings?"

"A copy of the drawings. They weren't signed. It wasn't exactly proof."

"But she thought it was proof."

"She did," Shane admitted. "And I didn't back her."

"Why am I not surprised?"

"It won't hold up in court. But it was enough for her. And, I guess that's good enough for me, too."

Jennifer's expression softened. "And you're here to tell her that."

"I am."

"Shane, are you in love with her?"

Shane knew he was. There was no other explanation.

He pictured Darci in that long, white dress again. Then he pictured her with a baby in her arms, Gus and Boomer frolicking on the mansion lawn. He wanted her, now and forever. And he was going to find a way to make that happen.

In fact, he *had* a way to make that happen.

He came to his feet. "Wouldn't that just solve everything?"

"Wouldn't what solve everything?"

"I marry her, and she'll instantly own half the company."

A grin stretched across Jennifer's face. "No prenup?"

The idea gained traction in his mind. "She could stop searching for the proof that probably doesn't even—"

It hit him then. Darci wasn't the type to give up. She was clever, and she was determined. If she hadn't come home, she was back at the mansion looking for the original drawings.

He coughed out a laugh.

"What?"

"She's back at the mansion right now. I'd bet money on it. She waited until I left, probably hiding in the shrubbery. And then she went back to search."

"So why are you smiling?"

"Because she's devious, and I love that about her. But I'm going to catch her red-handed, and I'm going to end this once and for all."

Darci groaned as she muscled the walnut desk away from the wall in Dalton Colborn's bedroom. She let her residual anger give her strength, and the heavy thing inched forward.

The housekeeper, Estelle, hadn't seemed at all surprised to see her return and had happily let her into the mansion. Darci hadn't felt any remorse as she headed straight upstairs to the master bedroom. Shane could have her arrested, for all she cared.

Maybe it would cause a scandal. Maybe there'd be reporters. Maybe she'd recant everything she said to Berkley Nash. Shane wasn't upstanding and professional. He was a cad. Bianca might have been right, after all.

Darci didn't love Shane. She wouldn't love Shane. She absolutely refused to love a man who would string her along like that.

There. That fixed that.

She'd checked each of the desk drawers, pulling them right out of the frame and turning them upside down to look at the bottoms. Then she'd crawled underneath the desk, checked every crack and crevice for secret compartments. So far, she'd found nothing. But she refused to say die.

As she pushed on the desk, she couldn't help taking in the mess she'd made of the room. Too bad. She'd take a jackhammer to the place if she thought it would help.

Creating enough room to maneuver behind the desk, she felt for anything out of the ordinary. The top overhung the back, creating a sort of lip and she sat down, craning her neck to see what was underneath.

Her last, faint hope was a secret compartment. She'd seen old furniture made that way. You pressed in just the right spot, and a panel opened up or a mini-drawer came free.

There had to be something here.

She could just barely make out a seam in the wood of one panel. She ran her fingers along it and came to a smooth indentation near the center. She pushed at the depression, and it wiggled. Squinting to see, she hooked her thumb in the groove and pulled forward. It gave, just a little, but it gave way.

She forgot about Shane's treachery and everything else as she came up on her knees, digging her fingernails into the crack. She pulled hard, and a sheet of wood slid out about an inch. Her heart rate doubled, her pulse pounding in her veins. She took hold of the thin panel with both hands and drew it forward.

The narrow compartment was filled with dust, but buried in the dust was a flat plastic bag. She pulled it out, sneezing from the cloud of particles that billowed into the air. She was sweating, and she pushed back her damp hair.

She went to where the light was better, finding a taped flap on the opaque plastic bag. She held her breath and peeled it open.

She slid out the papers, unfolded them, and there it was, the original set of schematic drawings. Her entire body sagged in relief.

Her heart pounding with excitement, she smoothed them out on the carpeted floor. They were nothing but shapes and lines and numbers, making no sense to her. But in a bottom corner, there was a date, along with her father's signature.

"Darci?" Shane's voice boomed in the doorway.

She popped her head up from behind the desk, excited to share the find with him, then remembering at the last second that he was a jerk, and she was furious.

He gaped at the awkward position of the desk, the scattered dust and the drawers strewn around the room. His shocked expression was almost comical. She tried to stay furious. She tried not to love him. But all she wanted to do was rush into his arms.

"Have you lost your mind?" he demanded.

She came to her feet. "You left me no choice."

"You *dismantled* my father's desk?"

"I had to."

"No." He gave his head a rapid shake. "You didn't have to."

The rhythm of their debate was familiar to her, in a good way. "I had to prove my point."

"You're trying to justify a crime spree?"

"It wasn't exactly a spree."

"I should have you arrested."

He was angry. He was bullheaded. And he was annoying. But it didn't seem to dampen her feelings for him, and she couldn't wait to tell him what she'd found.

"Shane, it's here—"

"But I won't have you arrested."

"Shane, it's—"

"I have a proposition for you instead. Well, more of a—"

"Stop talking, I—"

"No, you stop talking," he insisted.

"It's really important," said Darci.

"So is what I have to say."

"But—"

"Okay, now I'm thinking maybe I'll press the alarm button and have you arrested, after all."

Darci clamped her lips together.

"Good."

For some reason, he smiled at her. She opened her mouth to step into the silence, but he put an index finger across her lips.

He stepped in closer, his touch still light on her mouth. "I have an idea."

She lifted her brow.

"It's outside the box. But everything about our relationship has been outside the box."

She pursed her lips in frustration. What she had to tell him would have taken only a fraction of the time.

"You think you deserve half of Colborn."

That wasn't what she wanted. "I—"

"One more word, and I kiss you."

"I never once—"

He kissed her. Before she could make another sound, his lips were on hers, tasting sweet, familiar and, oh, so wonderful.

She couldn't hold out against him, and soon they were pressed tightly together. His arms wrapped around her, and the kiss went deeper and deeper.

After long, disorienting, satisfying minutes, he drew back. He framed her face with his hands, looking into her eyes.

"I love you, Darci. I'm in love with you, and I want you in my life forever."

The fight in her evaporated. "Huh?"

"The solution is so simple."

"Wait a minute. What?"

"You marry me."

Her brain scrambled to keep up with his words.

"You marry me, Darci, and half of Colborn is yours. It doesn't matter who invented what. It doesn't matter if we never prove anything. Though, I have to say, I'm definitely seeing your side of it right now."

"What?" she repeated.

"I'm seeing it your way."

"Not *that*."

"Oh, I'm asking you to marry me."

Not that, either. He loved her? He believed her?

She didn't know where to go first.

"I… You…" She gestured in the direction of the desk. "I found it, Shane."

He paused. "You found what?"

"The drawings. I found the original drawings."

"They exist?"

"There were two desks. They were identical. And there was a secret compartment. At the back of this one. I'm assuming they got mixed up somehow."

"Darci, I don't follow…"

She couldn't help but smile. "Come and look."

He followed her. She lifted the drawings, placing them on the desktop so they could both see.

He gazed at the documents.

"So, that's it then?" he asked.

Her chest tightened with a deep sense of satisfaction. "Mystery solved."

Her father's good name as an engineer was exonerated. He would take his rightful place in the history of the turbine engine. She might even be able to correct the patent.

"I guess you won't have to marry me." There was disappointment in Shane's tone.

"I won't have to marry you," she agreed. "But I do *want* to marry you."

"Say that again."

She rubbed her hand along his steel-hard biceps, loving the feel of him. "Not to get my hands on Colborn Aerospace. Not to clear my father's name. But because I love you, too."

"Oh, Darci."

"I'm in love with you, Shane. And I very much want to marry you."

He pulled her into his arms. "I can't believe it. You are the most amazing, gorgeous, tenacious, perfect woman in the world. I love you so much. I thought I'd lost you. I'm so glad I haven't."

She sighed, leaning up against him in complete contentment. "I bet our fathers could never have imagined this."

"I hope they're up there watching. And I hope they keep watching in amazement. Because we're going to do things with Colborn Aerospace that they never dreamed." He rubbed his hands along her back. "That is, unless you want to rename the company? Do you want to get your name in there, too?"

"I think that would be a bad business decision. You know, from a branding perspective."

"It probably is."

"Besides, I'll be a Colborn soon."

"Yes, you will. Just as soon as I can make it happen. You like Vegas?"

"You're not getting married in Vegas." Justin's voice unexpectedly joined the conversation from the doorway.

"Who let you in?" asked Shane.

Justin ignored the question. "I'm thinking a big, splashy wedding, where we invite hundreds of potential clients."

"Forget it," said Shane.

"Hi, Justin," said Darci, peeking from behind Shane's shoulder.

"You're not ticked at me?" Justin asked.

"I'm over it."

"Good." Justin moved into the room. "Because we're going to need to work together. We're not out of the woods yet, but this is a fantastic human-interest story. It'll reestablish Shane's good reputation and give us a launching pad for the new line of business. You can't buy this kind of publicity."

"Ignore him," Shane said to Darci.

"I don't think it's the worst idea in the world," said Darci.

"Very funny," said Shane.

"She's brilliant," said Justin.

"It almost seems fitting," said Darci.

Shane pulled back. "Tell me you're not serious."

"If it wasn't for Colborn Aerospace, we never would have met," said Darci. "You love the company. I love your plans for it. We both want nothing but the best for the employees. If getting married with a splash will help, I say we do it."

"You should listen to your fiancée," said Justin.

"She can have whatever wedding she wants," said Shane.

She patted his cheek with her palm. "As long as you're the groom, I really don't care about the details."

His gaze softened, and so did his voice. "You don't have to decide right now."

Darci turned to grin at Justin. "I've already decided. Go ahead and start planning."

Justin was out the door before Shane could disagree.

"Is this partnership going to be lopsided?" Shane asked her.

"This partnership is going to be perfect."

"Half the company, half the mansion, half of my bed."

"You wear the tiger-striped boxers."

"And you wear the diamond ring." He twined their hands together, stroking her left middle finger. "Right now. Let's go. We're sealing this deal today."

* * * * *

*If you loved this novel
by* USA TODAY *bestseller Barbara Dunlop,
pick up Riley's story, the second book in the*
CHICAGO SONS *series:*

*Men who work hard, love harder
and live with their fathers' legacies...
SEDUCED BY THE CEO*

Available June 2015 from Harlequin Desire!

*If you're on Twitter,
tell us what you think of Harlequin Desire!
#harlequindesire*